Block 11

Block 11

Piero degli Antoni

Translated by

Erin Waggener

St. Martin's Press 〰 New York

BLOCK 11. Copyright © 2012 by Piero degli Antoni. Translation copyright © 2012 by Erin Waggener. All rights reserved. Printed in the United States of America. For information address St. Martin's Press, 175 Fifth Avenue, New York, N.Y. 10010.

www.stmartins.com

ISBN 978-1-250-00102-3 (hardcover)
ISBN 978-1-250-01204-3 (e-book)

First published in Italy by Newton Compton editori under the title *Blocco 11*.

First U.S. Edition: October 2012

10 9 8 7 6 5 4 3 2 1

For my father, a partisan without ideologies,
who never lost sight of the right path

Block 11

"Wake up. Wake up, my darling."

The old man sleeping next to her opened his eyes with great effort.

"Mmm . . . what is it, *darling*?"

"It's time to get up. Today is the day, have you forgotten? Come on, I'll get breakfast ready."

The woman thrust the sheets aside with a force that allowed her feet to slide down toward the floor. With her soles planted firmly on the ground, she steadied her body, her weight on her elbow, bracing herself for the next step.

She was old and tired, and the maneuvering required simply to stand up grew more exhausting with each passing day.

For a moment, she stayed very still, allowing both the dizziness to pass and her heart rate to steady again. Behind her, still motionless, lay her husband, his eyes wide open. He too waited, in hopes that he would be seized by enough energy to get out of bed.

She counted silently. "One . . . two . . . three." By the time she reached ten, she told herself she would be on her feet. She found herself filled with an inexplicable sense of relief. For a moment she marveled at the unanticipated sensation. And then it suddenly made sense: there was hardly a need to rush; she could give herself all the time in the world she needed to get out of bed; it was assuredly a luxury that had not been afforded to her earlier in her life.

"Ten." With one deep breath she pulled herself up. She felt dizzy, but she would need only a few seconds before taking her first steps of the day. In just three or four small strides, she would reach the windowsill.

Just beyond those glass panes she'd find the streets of Brooklyn, saturated in the gray light of dawn. The view wasn't terribly magnificent—just little two-story houses, a corner tobacco shop, and a school in the distance. It seemed a world away from the Manhattan skyline, and yet she adored this little spot, where she knew no harm could come to her.

She turned toward the bed. Her husband was struggling to untangle himself from the sheets.

"Wait, let me help you."

She turned around and leaned toward him. She pulled off the sheets that had been wrapped around his feet. She lifted his frail ankles and helped him set his feet upon the floor. When he sat up, they found themselves face to face. They peered into each other's eyes, and for a split second, she spotted that cheeky look that had so enchanted her years ago.

The old man was finally seated on the bed, his back curved from the weight of time. His plaid nightshirt hung limply from his thin shoulders. Again she leaned toward him, holding him this time by his armpits. But as she attempted to pull him up, he quickly swatted her away.

"*A brokh!* First of all, I'm not that decrepit," he snapped. "And secondly, the day that I can't get my own self out of bed, I want you to call the police, tell them that I'm a criminal and that I was attacking you. Then, have them shoot me. And lastly, if you try to help me up again, you and I are both going to end up on the floor."

The woman smiled to herself.

He clung proudly to the headboard as he managed to set his own feet squarely on the floor.

"I'm going to the bathroom," he announced is if it were some sort of declaration of war. The woman made her way toward the kitchen, a tiny room that could hardly accommodate a single person at a time. She lit the stove under a pot, the contents of which had been prepared the night before. She opened one of the ancient white kitchen cupboards—they hadn't changed since the fifties—and pulled out the necessary accoutrements for a table setting. She set everything on a tray and brought it into the dining room, unquestionably the most beautiful room in the apartment, boasting wooden floors and ornate stucco molding. The walls gave way to three windows from which one could see the little neighborhood park. At the center of the room sat a long, narrow table, one which seemed fit more for a restaurant or a wedding banquet rather than a home. She quietly shuffled about the room in her green felt slippers, placing the tray that held the cutlery at the center of the table. She began to arrange the place settings. The bowls were all made of shoddy tin, resembling old mess-tins from the war. They were each misshapen leftover pieces; corroded in parts and dented in others. She placed them meticulously on the table, one after the other in a most precise manner. The first, the second, then the third . . . When she had finished, there were ten place settings in all. She carefully studied the table so as to ensure that the symmetry of each setting was not compromised. She returned to the kitchen. She observed the pot on the lit stove in which a blackish concoction now boiled. The old woman tasted it with a spoon, and then turned off the flame.

She opened another cupboard, and from it she pulled out a large paper sack. She took out a loaf of rye bread, which she painstakingly sliced with a serrated knife. The bread was old, and had become hard and fairly unappetizing. She sliced the loaf into ten equal portions, pausing after each one to ensure that the size was indeed the same as all the others. She set the slices in a basket and returned to the dining room. She examined the table yet again, placing a slice next to each tin bowl. She then carried the pot, in which the coffee still boiled, into the dining room, all the while teetering from the weight of the load. With an old distorted, wooden ladle, she poured a large serving into each tin. When the preparations were complete, her husband emerged from the bathroom freshly shaven and dressed in a white robe.

"You've already prepared everything," he mumbled, disappointed at not having helped her.

"Get changed and come in."

After a moment, the old man reappeared, dressed in a chestnut brown woolen suit. His pants, which were much too long, brushed the floor, and the cuffs of his oversized shirt peered out from beneath his jacket sleeves. At one time it had been quite an elegant suit, yet it now seemed somewhat ragged.

They each took their places: he seated himself at the head of the table, while she took the chair just to his left.

The old man tore a generous piece from his hardened slice of bread and dipped it in the ersatz coffee to soften the bite. His teeth were no longer what they used to be, yet he had no desire to succumb to the idea of dentures. In truth, he still felt very much like the same young man who had miraculously survived the depths of hell.

Cautiously, he bit into his stale morsel of bread, struggling to swallow. The old woman did the same.

The rest of the table was vacant. A faint line of steam rose from each of the other eight bowls before dissipating into the air, while the eight slices of bread remained, waiting patiently to be devoured. The old man ate another mouthful of bread and sipped a few spoonfuls of coffee. The smaller morsels seemed to please the old woman much more. They ate, consumed by a seemingly sacred silence, one that neither of them dared to break. Their eyes were lost in thought, filled by images both distant and terrible.

Ten minutes passed, and no one came to sit. The eight places remained empty. The steam no longer rose from the bowls: the black liquid had now turned cold. The old woman stared at their own empty tin bowls and the few crumbs that remained on the tablecloth.

"Are you done, *hartseny i*?" she asked him. Her husband nodded his head, and then got up from the table.

"Are you going to get ready then?" the old man asked his wife.

She shook her head. "I'm feeling quite tired this morning. You go. Tell the rabbi that I wasn't feeling well." He lingered there for a moment, surprised by her sudden break in routine.

"Are you sure?"

"You go. I'll prepare everything here, and maybe even have a bath. You'll come home for lunch, won't you?"

He was not sure whether a question mark followed her last words; nonetheless, he nodded his head. He then put on his coat and his outdated, wide-brimmed hat, one which he had worn with pleasure for the last thirty years, and turned to go.

And there, at the door, just as they had done every day for the last fifty years, they kissed each other on the cheek. The old man left without another word.

From the window of the descending plane, the man in the blue suit could see every detail of Kennedy Airport just below him.

The sky was perfectly clear, a rarity for New York City. The closer the plane's arrival came, the more he—a tall blond man with piercingly blue eyes, who, though in his sixties, still looked quite young even with a slight receding hairline—was overcome by apprehension. He had traveled more than five thousand miles and yet during those final minutes he wanted nothing more than to turn around and go back without ever touching the ground. That, however, was impossible. He knew he had to finish what he'd started more than a year ago.

He had to. Yes, it was a force greater than his own will. *He had to.* He had to go to New York and ring their doorbell. If he turned back now, he'd never again find the courage to try, and for that he'd never forgive himself. He needed closure on this part of his life, one that began more than fifty years ago. Otherwise he'd never find peace. One year had passed since life as he knew it had been completely transformed. All because of an arrival of a package from Germany. Never had he imagined that such a nondescript little package could have so drastically transfigured his life. A small parcel—no bigger than a shoe box—had managed to alter his entire existence.

There were many who said it was not he who bore the blame. He was innocent. And yet, just as a witness to a homicide might, he felt responsible for not having prevented it. He needed to be forgiven, and he hoped he had found the means to do so. No, it was not his fault, so many people had told him the very same thing, especially his wife. He didn't take part, *he was innocent.* But he certainly didn't feel that way. And just as his parents had taught him, *for better or worse,* he could not simply accept the gratifying moments in life and reject all the rest. Be it riches or debt, one either wholly accepts what they've inherited, or they accept nothing at all. He, however, had accepted what had been passed on to him, and for a year now that unbearable load had weighed heavy on his conscience. He had traveled all the way to New York in order to pay off a fifty-year-old debt. Whether or not he'd find a way remained unanswered, but he was certainly going to try.

The plane straightened out and headed in the direction of the tarmac. In a few moments, they would land in New York.

As the old man opened the synagogue's doors to leave, he was blinded momentarily by the bright sunlight. Squinting as he made his way, he took no notice of the blond gentleman on the other side of the street, who was dressed in a light blue suit with his jacket flapping in the wind. Next to him stood another man, an orthodox Jew, who was wearing both a *kippah* and a long *peot*. The two men spoke in hushed tones. Upon seeing the old man at the synagogue, the Jewish gentleman gestured in his direction. The blond man smiled and thanked him. The Jewish gentleman turned and continued on his way, yet the blond man did not; he lingered for a moment, his eyes fixed upon the old man on the other side of the street.

The old man took no notice. Taking the road toward home, he thought about what the rabbi had said. The routine prayers at the synagogue had not brought him much comfort that day. He had uttered the words to each prayer yet his thoughts had followed a different course entirely. It was as if his mind were trying to flee, and yet some force kept hurling it irretrievably back; like a barking dog who has escaped his cage yet is still bound by his chain. The sky above was a clear blue, while icy gusts of wind swept the streets below. Still the same cold weather. It was April, and yet spring seemed terribly distant. He looked down, as if unsure of himself. He stopped walking. Continue home? He really had no desire to. Not because of his wife, his dear, sweet beloved *libling*, but because of the sudden irresistible urge he felt to run away from everything, above all from himself.

In the distance he could hear a ferry sounding, and suddenly he had an idea; he could take the Staten Island Ferry, the same one visitors take to tour the harbor. How long had it been since the last time? Perhaps he'd never even taken the ferry. Those first years in New York hadn't been easy, he'd had no time, and then after . . . well, afterward there always seemed to be something else he'd had to do. A tour on the Staten Island Ferry, the perfect idea! Elated by the prospect, he raised his arm and flagged a passing taxi. A quarter of an hour later, he was at Whitehall Ferry Terminal.

He exited the car slowly and with difficulty, all the while thwarting the driver's attempts to help with an imperious swat of the hand. Once out of the cab, he looked ahead toward the pier. He was in luck: the boat was still docked and loading its last few passengers. The ferry would depart in only a few minutes time.

He passed through the terminal and made his way toward the ferry as quickly as he could.

He boarded the ferry. "We leave in ten minutes," the crewman informed him.

He made his way to the top deck, and found a seat out in the open air. He rubbed the sleeves of his thin jacket; it was going to be quite chilly, but he couldn't allow himself to miss such a glorious morning. The sunlight, the crisp air; these were exactly the things he needed to clear his mind of those dark thoughts. The plastic chairs which had been bolted to the floor were nearly empty. His sole company was a group of youngsters, presumably tourists, who were making quite a racket just a few feet away.

Moments later, just as had been announced, the ferry set sail. Their departure was accompanied by a throaty gurgle from the diesel motor as the boat accelerated. For a few seconds, a cloud of black, foul-smelling smoke from the boat's exhaust enveloped them before the wind carried away its last traces.

And just like that, he found himself in the middle of the harbor. The boat moved steadily away from the shore, bestowing to them a gradual but continuous change of scenery. Little by little, they traveled farther away, and the city gained scope bit by bit in varying detail, like an enormous puzzle that emerges fully as one piece at a time is added. The view lifted his spirits. And he did indeed, feel at peace.

The boat changed course, heading toward the Statue of Liberty. The wind blew at his back.

". . . zen. . . ."

Snippets of the conversation between the youngsters seated behind him were carried in by gusts of wind.

". . . sch . . . eutz . . . ."

He tried his best not to pay attention, but the syllables carried away by the wind resonated deep within. He tried to resist, to expunge them from his thoughts, until . . .

"Mützen ab!"

Moshe turned pale with shock. His heart came to a grinding halt like a rusted old piston.

"Mützen ab!"

A peal of laughter rang in his ears and collided against the distraught expression on the old man's face. Dazed, he turned around very slowly. The youngsters pushed and elbowed one another, all the while shouting and laughing. One boy, who was bigger than the rest, reached across the chairs, and with a quick swoop, snatched another boy's hat, lifting it in the direction of the Statue of Liberty.

"Mützen ab!" he shouted, and broke into a fit of laughter.

The old man sank further into his chair, clasping his hands over his ears to drown out the sounds. *Mützen ab, Mützen ab, Mützen ab.* He ground his teeth and shut his eyes, but the sounds would not let go of him. They held him in their clutches, and hurled him backward, ever further backward, into the deep abyss that was his past.

"Mützen ab!"

In anguish, the man looked at the petty officer, anxious to obey his orders, but unsure how to carry them out. The SS officer sensed his hesitation, and with the back of his hand, he sent the man's hat tumbling to the floor.

"Mützen ab!" he shouted again, inches from the man's face. Taking hold of the large baton he carried on his belt, the officer raised it above his head, ready to deal a fatal blow.

"Herr Oberscharführer, *einen Moment, bitte,"* came a voice from behind the soldier. The guard turned incredulously; no one ever dared to meddle in his affairs. Yet the moment he saw who had called his name, the SS officer's face broke into a smile.

"Ah, it's you, Moshe."

The prisoner who had spoken was neither tall nor particularly robust, yet there he stood, with a boyish grin stretching ear to ear. Unable to step out of line, the prisoner waited for the guard to approach. The guard glanced backward at the prisoner he was about to strike, and then slowly lowered his baton.

"Lève-toi ton bonnet, imbécile!" Moshe muttered in the direction of the other prisoner.

"What did you tell him?" the SS officer demanded with sudden suspicion.

"That *Mützen ab* translates to take off your hat, and that he ought to remember it well for the next time."

"These French are all such *Scheiße*. It's like they all have syphilis that's eating away at their brains."

Moshe shrugged. "It's not their fault. What would be on *your* mind if you had the Eiffel Tower right in front of your eyes day after day?"

The SS officer broke into a fit of laughter. With that, Moshe swiftly pulled a small object from beneath his striped uniform.

"Look," he whispered, opening his hand ever so slightly to allow the officer to see what lay within.

The SS officer paled with surprise.

"Where did you get that?"

"It's a trade secret."

"You know I could have you shot for this? I bet you 'procured' this from Kanada."

Moshe held open his hand so that the officer could take the brown cylindrical object. The SS guard seized it and held it to his nostrils. He inhaled quickly and deeply, and then tucked it safely in his jacket pocket.

"It's a real Montecristo all right, but why don't you smoke it yourself?"

"Well, first, the flavor is far too strong for my liking. Second, I prefer cigarettes. And third, smoking a cigar might be a tad obvious for a fellow like myself, don't you think? That's why I thought of you."

The SS officer spun on his heels, turning in the direction of the French prisoner, who immediately began to tremble with fear.

"When I say *Mützen ab*, you remove your hat, is that understood?" he yelled.

The man nodded his head in frantic agreement, despite having not understood a single word. The SS officer looked the prisoner over with a dubious eye, grabbed hold of his baton and dealt him a single blow to the back, though not with a great amount of force. The French prisoner took the blow with a painful grimace.

"Good. Now I'm sure you fully understand," said the soldier. "If you do not obey, the next time I will make your brains come out your ears."

The Frenchman waited until the officer had moved a suitable distance away before turning toward Moshe, his face showing a smile twisted by pain.

"*Merci!*" he whispered.

"Don't fool yourself," Moshe responded in French, without bothering to turn his head. "You would have been better off if he had smashed your head in. Only an idiot doesn't know that *Mützen ab* is the first thing one must learn in here. The jackboots are in command; they care about their salutes. Hats off and then hats on, hats off and then hats back on. They go mad for it. And we comply. Regardless, I only got involved because otherwise the *Appellzahl* would have started over again, and we've already been here for hours."

The streets outside their blocks were crowded with thousands of men. The sun was setting and the guards in the watchtowers had already turned on the high-beam searchlights, giving the impression that daylight was returning, as the beams of light cast rays upon the camp, framing the crowds of prisoners into geometric displays. The chain of human beings covered the entirety of the scale between life and death; the latter being nothing more than skeletons covered in skin—eyes bulging out from within their cavernous sockets, their gazes empty and lifeless. They were the so-called Muslims.* Just above them on the survival scale were other people with meager frames, showing only a hint of flesh on their bones here and there. All of them encased in their striped uniforms—or even civilian clothes with the black-and-white-striped patch sewn onto the backs—all of them with their hair shaved down to the roots by electric shavers, and all with clogs of one type or another, even odd pairs, all covered in mud and ice. They had been standing there for three hours, lashed by the icy cold winds despite it already being April, while the Kapos counted and recounted each detainee before fearfully relaying their numbers to the SS officers. And every time the Kapos would be sent back, they were forced to count once more.

Despite the fatigue, the hunger, the thirst, the cold, and the numbness of their hands, nobody dared to move. Absolute immobility was a must. Suddenly, a few rows behind Moshe, a weakened, middle-aged man collapsed to the ground. Moshe turned his head in effort to catch a hurried glance; he then quickly reassumed his position. With a flash, the Prominent and his attendants rushed over. Jerking the poor man upright, they stood him on his feet. But the man swayed back and forth, and once again crumpled to the ground. Yet again, the officers hauled him to his feet, supporting him beneath his armpits while giving him a few sharp strikes to the buttocks. Yet despite all this, the man still fell to his to knees, unable to stand on his own. In response, the officers screamed in his face and beat him repeatedly. The man accepted the beating without any reaction.

Suddenly, an SS officer appeared before them. Moshe knew

---

* Term used to denote the weakest prisoners fated for death. Its origin stems from the religious practice in which prayer is carried out while one is on his or her knees; these prisoners, too weak to work, remained on their knees.

exactly who he was and had always made a point to stay out of his way; he was not one of those SS officers whose mercy could be bought with a packet of cigarettes or a gold watch, or even a pair of lady's silk underwear that could be given to the camp prostitutes. No, he was one of those fanatical Nazis without a trace of humanity.

The German officer shoved the Kapos out of the way, and grabbed his baton from his belt. It was an elegant baton made of dark wood and of illustrious origin, one that had clearly belonged to a rich Jewish inmate and had been stolen from Kanada. He held it high above the kneeling man, ready to strike. Moshe had been following from out of the corner of his eye, made possible by ever so slight movements of his head. The Unterscharführer froze at the last moment; something or someone had distracted him. Lowering his baton, he turned to look at the person standing next to the man in line.

"You," he said.

He had turned to face a boy of no more than eighteen years old, perhaps even younger, for there were many young people who had lied about their age in an attempt to flee the *kremchy*. The boy turned toward the SS guard, desperately trying not to express any emotion in his face.

"You," the SS repeated, "are his son, correct?"

The boy gave a slight yet barely discernible reaction as a hint of surprise flitted across his face.

"Yes, *mein Herr*."

"Well, then take it!" The SS officer thrust the baton toward the boy's face. The young boy hesitated.

"Take it!" the officer ordered once more.

The boy stretched out a trembling hand, lightly brushing the baton's handle.

"Take it!"

The boy obeyed. He took hold of the baton as if it were a strange object. He stared inquisitively at the SS officer.

"Now strike him!"

It was only then that the boy fully understood. The SS meant for him to beat his father, on his knees beside him.

"Hit him!"

The young boy looked around, searching for help in vain. The other detainees remained stock-still; their stares vacant. One of the Kapos sneered without restraint. The only sound was the whistling of the wind.

"Hit him!"

The man suddenly came to, now fully comprehending the weight of the situation. With superhuman effort, he forced himself to stand once again on his own two feet, under the silent stares of the SS officer, the camp commanders, and all those around him. He swayed in the wind like a thin sheet of metal. Just when he looked as if he were to collapse once more, he managed to steady himself and stay upright.

The SS officer glared at the father and his son, taken aback by this sudden development. He wasn't sure what to do. He reached out his open hand. "The baton. Give it back to me."

The boy released his grip on the baton handle, in such a way that the SS officer could take back the weapon. Without sound, the crowd of inmates released a collective sigh of relief.

The German officer took hold of the baton, tapping it gently on the palm of his hand. And then he turned his focus to the man.

"Take it," he ordered, pushing the baton toward him.

The man, already exhausted from standing and shaking with fear, could only look on vacantly.

"Take it!"

The man tilted his head questioningly. But then he found the strength to take the baton that the officer had thrust upon him.

"And now strike him!" the officer ordered, indicating the man's son.

The man thought he had misheard. His eyes went wide with shock.

"He disobeyed an order from an SS officer. Now beat him!"

The man murmured something softly. Moshe couldn't understand what he said.

"Hit him!" the SS officer roared.

The man raised the baton as far as he could manage, and dealt a feeble blow to his son's back. And then his hands dropped to his sides, motionless. In another world, at another time, he would have cried. But all his tears had been exhausted. Moshe had never seen anyone cry in the camp.

"Hit him!"

The young boy found the courage to speak. "Hit me, Father. Come on, hit me, you needn't be afraid!"

The man began to sob. The baton swung harmlessly in his hand.

The SS officer took his pistol from his holster and pointed it at the man's head. "Strike him! Strike him or I will kill you both!"

The man didn't move. His kept his eyes on the ground.

"Hit him!" The SS officer had lost control and shouted maniacally.

Moshe averted his gaze. A few seconds later he heard a shot fired. Silence. And then another shot.

Addressing the Kapos, the SS officer spoke once more, his voice now steady and calm.

"Take them away . . . and call the officers at HKB."

The Kapos and his attendants took the bodies by their hands and legs and dragged them away. Nobody watched. All the prisoners who had been near the father and son in line stood motionless, not even a head turned. One of the prisoners nearby had been splattered by the blood from the shots. The single drop that had landed on his head now ran slowly down over his forehead. But he made no attempt to wipe it away, for during the roll call it was imperative to stay absolutely still, no matter what may happen.

"They are incensed today, these jackboots," Moshe mumbled quietly without turning to the man beside him, a Jewish man from Thessaloniki.

"I heard that three prisoners escaped," the other man answered, barely opening his mouth. Within the walls of the KZ, everyone learned to speak like a ventriloquist.

"Yeah, that's what they're saying. It doesn't bode well for us. They're even saying that they escaped from our barrack."

"Foolish . . . reckless . . . criminals . . ." whispered the Greek man furiously in his own tongue, still barely moving his lips. "Don't they know that now we will pay the price for their escape?"

Moshe shrugged. "They were only trying to save their own lives, just like everyone else in here. If you had the chance, wouldn't you do the same?"

The Greek was silent, troubled. His brooding thoughts were interrupted, however, by the long, piercing sound of a siren. The howling noise rose in a crescendo, holding on to the last screeching note for a minute before finally stopping. Moshe smiled to himself, knowing what it signified. In a flash, the camp burst into activity; hundreds of SS officers came running from every direction, scores of their guard dogs in tow.

"Look," Moshe whispered once more. "Here comes the head commandant."

The Sturmbannführer, the Kommandant of the KZ, got out of his Opel and stood before the inmates in the space that was allocated to the orchestra at the start and end of every day. He stepped up to the wooden podium, and looked out across the mass of doomed men; quiet and still beneath his gaze. Even without a loudspeaker, the silence coupled with the wind meant that his voice carried to every part of the camp, all the way to the last row of prisoners.

"At roll call today, three prisoners were missing from camp. We have reason to believe that they have attempted to escape. If they are caught, they will be shot. If they are not found, however, we will hold responsible all those prisoners who should have alerted us to their intentions and did not. They will be shot in their place. This will serve as a warning to any who might attempt to escape. You must all understand that an escape signals death for your fellow inmates."

"Dirty bastards!" the Greek man muttered beside Moshe, though Moshe couldn't tell if he was referring to the Germans or the inmates who had escaped.

The Sturmbannführer quickly descended from the performance platform, returned once again to his Opel, and was gone.

The camp transformed into a scene of frenetic activity, as was the case any time there was an escape attempt. Guard patrols would go both beyond the camp towers and into the grounds outside the camp, areas that were usually left unpatrolled. For three days and three nights the camp, lit up as if it were day, would be scoured from end to end as every angle and corner was searched. The hunt for the escapees had begun.

"*Absperren!*"

The roll call had ended. The inmates were now able to move so they could find their way back to their respective barracks. The exhausted prisoners traipsed across the unruly ground, their clogs sinking into the mud with every step. At times, they were forced to stop and free their shoes from the muddy mess that swallowed them. In doing so, their feet, marked by welts, scabs, and pus, took a beating. It would have been much easier to simply remove the shoes altogether and walk barefoot, but the SS officers would severely punish any prisoner who attempted any such action.

While at Kanada, Moshe had managed to procure a pair of quality leather shoes, and as such, he walked untroubled beside the Greek inmate, who struggled mightily to keep walking.

"Aristarchos, do you know who the inmates were who escaped?"

The Greek man only swore softly under his breath, adding nothing more.

The inmates around Moshe arrived at their barrack, number twenty-four, in silence. There, the group split as each inmate scurried toward his own pallet in a great rush of bodies.

Moshe lay down on his own mattress on the lowest bunk. The smell of the sleeping mat was nauseating. Some of the Muslim inmates above Moshe would often not be able to control their faculties, and would urinate and defecate throughout the night without even trying to get up and go outside. It was one of the major disadvantages of being on the lowest bunk. Yet, being on the bottom made it easier to get up and go to the bathroom during the night to pass all the water they had ingested from their daily soup ration. Another advantage was that Moshe was always one of the first to get to the *Wasserraum* in the morning for their brief, daily wash. This also meant that they avoided the inevitable thrashings that the *Blockältester* would dole out to anyone slow to move toward the line. Overall, Barrack 24 had a somewhat soporific atmosphere; the body heat from all the inmates created an almost tangible warmth.

In the weeks prior, as the Russian troops neared their camp, their rations had become increasingly more dissatisfying. The *Wassersuppe* they were given each day seemed to be ever more watery, and the precious pieces of turnips and potatoes seemed to diminish with every serving.

And yet, if a slice of meat happened upon their tin plates it sent a chill through each of the detainees. The origin of those suspect pieces was something that no one wanted to imagine.

Moshe heard the bells toll yet again, marking another day at the KZ. He knew that soon the soup would arrive. This knowledge prevented him from being surprised when the doors finally swung open. Yet, it was not the Kapo's assistants who arrived carrying the usual cauldron, but rather three SS men.

"Aufstehen!"

The prisoners leaped from their beds and scurried to their feet.

An Untersturmführer pulled a sheet of paper from his jacket pocket and unfolded it. In a monotone voice he began to recite a list of numbers.

"A-7713."

Each number called out by the SS was met by impenetrable silence. The detainees knew well what this list meant. Moshe followed along with detached interest, his constant exploits of various sources made him rather indispensable and therefore untouchable. One by one the numbers were called out. Moshe tried to identify the men. Many of the men he already knew. The others he spotted merely by way of their reaction.

They called Elias, a Polish rabbi—a man so defiant in his faith that throughout Yom Kippur he had fasted, rejecting the only good that could be found within the walls of the KZ.

There was also Jan, an extremely elderly Muslim who had managed to subsist until now, but who would undoubtedly soon be called. There was Otto, a short and stocky man who was respected by a great many. Branded a "Red Triangle" he never missed an opportunity to discuss the dealings of the proletariat and the revolution during the ephemeral periods of rest (one afternoon every other Sunday). Berkovitz also remained. He was a tall thin Jewish gentleman with a penetrating and yet detached stare. It was said that he came from rather substantial means. Berkovitz had somehow managed to keep his round metal-framed glasses.

The officer called the number of one of the prisoners who had only recently arrived. He was a tall and rather lanky boy with whom Moshe had not been acquainted. There was a break in the SS officer's recital of the registry. He had stopped, as if unable to make out the next set of numbers. In truth, there was little light inside the barracks.

"116.125."

It was Aristarchos's number! Moshe spun around in the direction of his Greek friend. On the man's face, Moshe could see his shock quickly transform into desperation. Aristarchos turned to Moshe, as if in some vain attempt to seek help or in the least to be consoled by an explanation. Yet time afforded no such request, and the SS officer carried on with the registry. Three sets of numbers remained.

The first number belonged to Alexey, a Ukrainian brute who was an aide to the Kapos. He was tall and quite robust thanks to the food rations he stole from the Muslims. Branded a "Green Triangle," in truth, he was nothing more than a common criminal who relished terrorizing the other detainees with cruel and violent acts. Moshe had not anticipated this selection. Still, it came as no great surprise. Life for the *Blockältesten* and the *Stubenältesten* was quite precarious. While there were obvious advantages, such as better food and little or no work, they were expected, in return, to institute and maintain perfect discipline within the barracks, which was achieved through cruelty and terror. For any offense or any mistake, they were swiftly replaced, punished, or even worse—as was the case when a prisoner escaped—these men were executed in their place. Even the most affable *Kapos* were forced to become nothing short of ferocious.

The ninth name called was that of the barrack leader, another "Green." He was both a cold and calculating man with whom Moshe had managed to concoct a series of profitable exchanges. Hearing his number came as little shock. It was natural to assume that he too would be selected alongside his aide.

Yet it was the last number that sent Moshe into a flurry of fright.

"76.723."

Moshe Sirovich.

There was not time enough to think. The SS ordered all those called to file into a line. They complied in silence. To flee now would be impossible. They exited the barracks, marching two by two. The officer marched at the forefront as the others tailed from behind, rounding out the sad procession of men. They advanced in the direction of the notorious Block 11. Two other guards were already present, directing a prisoner from one of the other barracks into the block. In the muted light, the prisoner's features seemed familiar to Moshe: it was Jiri, a "Pink Triangle" who had the misfortune of gaining a reputation for having allegedly been spotted alone with one of the *Blockältesten*. He was small in stature and had a dark complexion, and not a single hair on his body. His movements, as was his gait, were both svelte and ambiguous.

Moshe dreaded the thought of ending up in one of the detention cells set up under the stairway to the tunnels. The space, it was said, was no bigger than that of a dog kennel, much too narrow to lie flat and much too short to stand upright. When things went well, those inmates were given a bowl of soup a day. No light permeated within the cell walls. There was no water. Nor was there a toilet; the prisoner was forced to live in his own excrement.

Moshe breathed a sigh of relief; he soon realized he would be sent to one of the other cells; which would be only marginally larger, with a grate that would allow a faint glimmer of light to enter.

It was not uncommon for the SS to amass many prisoners at once into a single cell. This time, however, each of the prisoners was separated from the others. It was, no doubt, a strategic move administered by the commander, perhaps as an attempt to avoid one too many solitary escape attempts from merging into a communal one. Or perhaps it was simply by chance.

For a while, Moshe had led himself to believe that he had secured the benevolence of the SS officers, the *Blockältesten,* and the *Kapos* thanks to his many favors. It was only now that he discovered that he had deluded himself.

He knew there was only one way out of Block 11. Death.

The commander exited his Opel and entered the house. He made his way up to the loft that had been converted into an office. The wooden floors creaked with every step and the walls were covered by a tapestry that was peeling along the edges. The furnishings consisted only of a Biedermeier table, a grandfather clock, and a few modern chairs. On the table sat a chessboard.

He paused for a moment in front of the window, a spot that afforded a view of the entire camp illuminated by the floodlights from the watchtowers. He needed both silence and solitude in order to burn off the tensions that had accumulated throughout the morning. The sky was a dull gray; it was difficult to imagine that spring was quickly approaching. In moments such as these, he found himself nostalgic for the Bavarian sunshine and the brilliant white of the snowcapped mountains. The lightning-quick war that the Führer had promised now seemed to stretch out interminably.

Karl Breitner spun on his heels, startled by a noise. Behind him stood his wife, Frieda. She had ash-blond hair and a petite, yet well-proportioned frame. She wore a long, brown gabardine dress that came to just below her knees. A thin belt was neatly wrapped around her waist and on her feet were a pair of mid-high heels. She wore the party's emblem on her chest. The commander welcomed her with a smile and then turned once again toward the window. Standing behind him, she wrapped her arms around her husband.

"What's the matter?"

Breitner was quiet. He was never keen to admit defeat. Still, the situation would not permit him to stay silent forever.

"It seems that three prisoners have escaped."

With a sudden anxious tug, Frieda spun him around. Her eyes were wide.

"Escaped? But how——?"

"We don't know that yet. If we don't find them we'll shoot ten others in their place."

Frieda was visibly shaken by the news.

"So many have already escaped this year. The Reichsführer won't be happy."

"At the moment, Berlin has other things to worry about."

His wife stood, biting her lip in exasperation.

"You've always been good at what you do. This is a delicate situation, I'm sure. Were they Jewish?"

"Red Triangles."

The response calmed her.

"Do you have other news?"

"The eastern front is advancing. I spoke with one of the Wehrmacht officials last night. They're saying we won't make it through the end of the year."

"Don't say that!" Frieda's face flushed red with agitation. "You mustn't even think that way! The Führer will lead us to victory. How can you possibly doubt it? They'll need only one strategic retreat to execute the counteroffensive. Have you not read what Goebbels wrote in the *Völkischer Beobachter?* Our factories are in the midst of supplying us with new lethal armaments. By the end of the year we'll be advancing as far as Moscow! Our *Großdeutschland* will stretch from the Atlantic as far as the Ural Mountains!"

"No, of course, Frieda. It's just that there are moments—"

"Do you want to go back to Munich to work for Steinman in that little dump of an office? Have you forgotten what those conniving Jews did to you?"

Her eyes flushed with hatred.

"Have you forgotten how they worked your father into such horrid debt, and how they continued to feed him funds only to keep him beholden to them?"

Breitner remembered vividly. He thought of the villa in Munich where he had spent his childhood, amid the nightly grand soirees, the dozens of guests, and the cases upon cases of champagne on ice. Through the crack of the door left ajar, he could still make out the shimmering wrappings of the gifts brought by the guests. It left him with the sensation that his childhood must have been a joyous one. Mom and Dad were so very lovely.

"And have you forgotten what they did to your father, those *Jews*?"

How could he have forgotten? One morning an officer came to the house with the news that the property would be appropriated. That day they seized both the house and the tavern.

Only later would Karl discover that his father's immense debt no longer permitted him to live within his desired means. It was during the same year that the economy of the Weimar Republic had begun to fall into despair. After two years they had lost everything—the house, their savings, the business—and when they found themselves living in a fetid little apartment on the outskirts of town, Breitner's father had killed himself. A pistol to the mouth.

"They're the ones to blame, those *Jews*! They forced you to work in that horrid little place and carried on as if they had done you a favor! 'Mr. Breitner, we're so deeply sorry for your loss. Oh, so terribly sorry.'" Frieda carried on, in a querulous and false tone. "'We can, however, offer you a position that might be better suited to your academic capacities. It is not much for a person of your professional standing, but it's all we have.' You were at that desk tending to their accounts for twelve hours a day so that their decadent habits continued uninterrupted while we barely managed. But that's all over now. You finally have what you deserve. Just remember, the only thing for us in Munich is that miserable little two-room apartment."

She shook her arm in a manner that made her diamond bracelet slide from beneath her dress sleeve down to her wrist. She eyed it regretfully, as if she had suddenly been asked to hand it over.

"We have two gardeners, three housemaids, and a nursemaid. Every Saturday evening without fail we send a token of our appreciation along with a bottle of champagne to every officer within the camp. Would you have had all of this in Munich, Karl? You mustn't forget, Karl. You mustn't forget everything they did to your father. It is for this that we must be triumphant. It is for this reason that we must win. And for our son. So that we may be able to give him a life of peace and prosperity."

Frieda's eyes were blazing with emotion. Breitner pulled her close, kissing her and wrapping her in a tender embrace.

Indeed, she was right. He needn't be swayed by the defeatist nonsense written by those imbeciles in the Wehrmacht. There was no doubt that the Führer would lead them to a final victory. Nothing could withstand the power of the Third Reich. He simply needed to stay calm during these difficult moments and follow orders. And all would be well.

After a brief moment, Breitner withdrew his arms from around his wife. "Have you already eaten? Shall we then? It's almost ten o'clock."

A smile radiated from Frieda's face. She took him by the arm and together they made their way down the stairs.

"I made meatballs. Your favorite. With all this madness, I thought you'd have quite an appetite. Those three fools who escaped even managed to make you late for dinner."

For three days Moshe had been incarcerated in Block 11 and his hopes had been replaced with uncertainties. Still, he reveled in the prospect of the prisoners' escape and, moreover, the taste of triumph against the unassailable SS officers. When it came to matters of organization and discipline, the Germans were without equal, and yet it was these qualities that left them ill prepared in the face of any unanticipated incident. Still, Moshe knew that his life would be spared only if the escapees were captured. Only then would the ten hostages be freed. Then again, perhaps they would not: the SS officers often seemed swayed more by impulse than order. One thing was certain; there would be no tribunal to hear his appeals.

During those days Moshe relied on only one of his senses: his hearing. Pressed against the brick wall he sought out any noise that might reveal some detail of the ongoing search. Once in a while, he could make out the scuffling of feet, the barking of the dogs, or the roar of a commanding officer bellowing an order. It was difficult to keep track of time: only the arrival of the daily soup rations allowed him to separate one day from the next. One cup, two cups, three cups. . . . There was, however, a moment when he thought he heard an officer exclaim: "Abandon your posts!"

The officer roared his order louder yet again and again. After a moment his voice began to taper off into the distance. The order, which had been directed at the outer watchtowers closest to the commander's post, forced the guards to abandon their stations and return inside the camp walls. This left the area outside of the camp completely devoid of any surveillance. It was, in a sense, a momentary declaration of defeat. Having abandoned their search for the fugitives, the SS officers within the KZ returned once again to their routine surveillance duties. In truth, the area had been under such close watch. It would have been difficult to reach the *Generalgouvernement* without encountering patrols of any type. Moreover, many of the Poles in the area were anti-Semites: they would have undoubtedly informed the German authorities that a Jewish prisoner was on the loose.

When the cell door flung open, Moshe hadn't time enough to reflect on what was to come. The SS officer peered in, grimacing from the putrid stench that emanated from the small room.

"*Los!* Come out immediately."

Once outside, Moshe was forced to close his eyes, he was no longer accustomed to the harsh afternoon light. Once his pupils adjusted he realized he was standing alongside the other nine condemned prisoners. Each of their faces bore the same frightened expression, except for the Kapo and Jan, whose faces were perpetually indecipherable.

"Line up!" ordered the SS. The prisoners obeyed. They now understood that the escapees had managed to flee, and they knew death awaited them in return. As was usually the case, the punishment was ruled by the whims of the SS officers. In the early days of the KZ, the commander left the condemned prisoners to starve to death. Moshe recalled an enormous Polish man who, without food or water, had managed to survive for a month. After that, the SS had adopted other methods. They organized large-scale executions, complete with ominous gibbets, which sat in wait on the *Appellplatz*. They beat prisoners, and forced other detainees to join in, silently assisting in the macabre ceremony. These men were later forced to file across in front of the condemned who either lay dead or dying in agony. Moshe had once been chosen to assist in the execution of a *pipel*: a boy, much lighter than a grown man, who had resisted for more than half an hour. Moshe stood present watching as the boy hung by a rope; his eyes fluttering, his body trembling and thrashing in the air. The sight was enough to disturb even the SS officers.

It was sometimes the case that the officers themselves lacked the will or desire to properly orchestrate the mandated execution. It was in such instances that a simple shot to the back of the neck sufficed. Other instances involved sending the condemned to the *Revier,* where a nurse would administer an injection to the heart containing carbolic acid. If these methods were not accessible, the SS was obliged to carry out the standard punishment; twenty-five blows to the back. The execution methods were always erratic and unpredictable, which made them all the more frightening.

The SS officers escorted the prisoners into the shower quarters.

"Undress! *Los!*"

The prisoners obeyed. They removed their jackets, their pants, and lastly their grimy and pitiful underwear. They placed each of their garments on a washbasin: the clothing needed to remain intact for other prisoners, and the heat from the lead bullets would assuredly leave punctures in the garments. The nude prisoners were then led out of the barrack. The icy Polish wind caused the men to tremble with cold. Just outside of Block 11 lay the execution wall. Had the commander opted for a swift end, they would be directed there. Had they, however, been led toward the

Appellplatz, they would be taken to the gallows to be hung. Moshe knew that each of the other prisoners was consumed by this same thought. A few minutes of indecision passed. A small squad of SS officers, armed with rifles, stood at port arms in the yard between Block 10 and 11. At the exit, the officer turned right, and headed toward the wall. Moshe was sure they would meet their end in a few minutes.

"Herr Kommandant!"

The voice thrust Breitner back into reality. He lowered his gaze, eyeing a chessboard which lay on the table between himself and the Rapportführer. The officer eyed him with uncertainty.

"The knight, sir. I moved the knight." He pointed to the piece as if to clarify the game's configuration for the commanding officer.

The Kommandant heaved a sigh of tedium and moved the bishop to the far end of the board. "Check," he announced. "Mate," he added after a short pause. The officer had fallen victim to one of the more elementary gaffs of the game. Any decent player, expert or otherwise, would have spied it at first glance.

"Herr Rapportführer, you are a most expert officiator, and a most skilled strategizer, whose scorekeeping is most accurate. But"—he hesitated—"as far as chess players go, you are quite the mediocre opponent. Most mediocre, indeed."

The Rapportführer sprang nervously to his feet.

"My apologies sir, I regret not being able to offer you a more formidable challenge. I assure you I will seek to better employ my services the next time. And now, if you'll excuse me, sir."

He discharged a military salute, and turned to exit.

Breitner dismissed him with a solitary gesture. He watched as the Rapportführer passed through the courtyard of Block 11 with quick, furious steps. Poor presumptuous idiot. Was he truly convinced that Breitner would recommend him to the Reichsführer to be promoted? Imbecile. He interlaced his fingers, turned his palms outward and extended his arms in a stretch; it was a gesture that seemed to have a calming affect.

In that very instant, the cell door to Block 11 opened. The naked prisoners emerged one by one, alarmed and disoriented, squinting in the face of the harsh light.

Ah, of course, thought Breitner, the ten hostages taken after the escape. The reminder brought with it a certain sense of fatigue. For three days, the camp had been on high alert without uncovering a trace of the fugitives. With or without the runaways, punishment was necessary. The only way to prevent continual criminal attempts was to carry out the very penalty that was to be reserved for the runaways. Executing their families and friends was indeed the most effective form of retribution.

The commanding officer impassively eyed the ten hostages. Each one was thin and haggard, the bones of their weakened frames shone through their skin. For Breitner, they were nothing more than part of a subhuman entity, which, at the present, was necessary for the advancement of the Reich. However, in the coming months they would be phased out and extinguished entirely. There was no hatred or anger within him: he simply held the conviction that an inferior race was destined to make way for that which was stronger.

The ten had amassed in a frenzied heap in front of the wall, as if each one sought to protect themselves from the others. They had silently resigned themselves to a state of passive resistance and waited to hear the final orders called.

Breitner heaved a sigh as he waited for the sounds of gunfire. With listless effort, he gathered the mound of files that lay before him on the table. He himself had chosen these ten men, just three days ago. He opened the folders, absently thumbing through each one. A politician, a Jew renowned for trafficking, another rich Jew, a common criminal who, like so many others, had become a *Blockältester*. . . . In the end, it was all the same filth that would be eradicated for the good of the Third Reich.

Breitner lifted his gaze. The SS officers were lining the men against the wall in military fashion. The execution needed to be carried out in a manner that prevented unnecessary misspending of ammunition; the commandant waited in anticipation of the shots that would mark the end of the exercise.

Moshe scoured the faces of the SS officers who, in a short moment, would fulfill their duty as his executioners. He sought in vain to unearth a hint of humanity upon their faces, yet he was met with only cold, hardened, empty expressions, which arduous training and discipline had irrevocably etched into their skin.

The SS officers gripped their firearms, aiming at each prisoner's chest. One more minute and it would all be over. Moshe stood with his eyes tightly shut; he did not have the courage to look his own death in the face. Heroic feats of that kind had always seemed absurd, and moreover, useless. His only wish was that it would all end soon.

He heard the sounds of the rifles, each cocking into position. "Stop!"

Moshe's eyes flew open. A guard came running toward them from the direction of the gestapo's headquarters.

"Stop!" the guard shouted, frantically waving his hand through the air while straining to keep from slipping in the mud that seemed to cover every surface.

The platoon's chief officer turned around, taken aback by the soldier's orders. After a moment's hesitation, even the armed and readied soldiers turned and yielded to curiosity.

"Stop!" the guard invoked once more, despite having already caught the attention of the platoon. The now vexed petty officer anxiously tapped his boot on the ground, waiting to hear the cause of such an interruption.

"Well?" he asked once the guard arrived within earshot.

The guard, looking somewhat sheepish, gave a military salute and began his explanation. 'The commander has ordered an immediate suspension of the execution, sir . . ." Moshe felt a sudden rush of heat fill his veins, spreading into even the most minute capillaries in his body. *Suspend the execution.*

"The commander has ordered that you wait here with the prisoners. He is on his way, sir."

Each of the detainees remained motionless, paralyzed with fear like a hunted animal hoping to elude its predator. There they stood, naked and immobile, with inaudible labored breaths, each one avoiding the gaze of the SS officers. They wanted only to disappear, to vanish, to be invisible. They desired nothing more than to never have to return to their stinking, overcrowded barracks.

Ten minutes passed; the office door to the gestapo's headquarters opened and from it exited the commander. Moshe's eyes drifted upward from the floor. He had seen Breitner on a few other occasions; he had often suspected that a shipment of watches and jewelry that he himself had prepared from Kanada had, in truth, been prepared for Breitner. At each of his sightings, Moshe took note of the subtle differences between the Sturmbannführer and the SS officers. Breitner wore a meticulously tailored uniform. Moshe was somewhat well versed in the field, and could spot its quality at first glance. Yet, it was not only his uniform that set him apart from the others. Breitner walked with an impeccable military gait, one which conveyed a certain subtle elegance. He exuded an air of regimented discipline and the elegance of a gentleman one might find along the promenade of Unter den Linden in Berlin.

The soldiers stretched their arms in a taut salute.

"Heil Hitler!"

The platoon's commanding officer seemed at once irritated and yet consumed with curiosity.

"Herr Oberscharführer," Breitner conferred.

Without further explanation, he turned and addressed the captives. His voice carried an unmistakable militaristic tone, and yet he spoke without raising his voice. "You should have been executed."

Moshe heaved a sigh of relief. He understood German quite well and recognized the conditional tense in his message.

"Yet, I've decided to give you a second chance. Minister Speer has expressed his interest in placing the strengths of each camp at the disposal of the Third Reich, and it has come to my attention that among you are quite a few excellent craftsmen."

He paused a moment. Complete and utter silence surrounded him. The sky was beginning to darken and take on the colors of night.

"Nine of you will be spared. Only one will be executed."

The hostages could not restrain themselves; each one peered with inquisitive apprehension toward the others. Moshe looked over at the elderly prisoner. Would they take Jan? Would it be Aristarchos? Or the Kapo? Or his aide? Or would they kill Moshe himself? Even the commander had to have known of his crucial "work" within the confines of the camp. The ever-growing heap of luxury goods that had accumulated at Kanada had found its way to their hands thanks entirely to Moshe.

The commander spoke by alternating his speech with lengthy

silent refrains, in which he took obvious pleasure. "As of yet, I have *not* decided who is to be executed."

Moshe, despite being quite proficient in German, suddenly felt as if he had misunderstood the commander's last words. And yet the utterance of "*nicht*" could not have been clearer: the commander had *not* yet chosen the inmate to be condemned.

A smile spread across Breitner's face. "I will leave that to you to decide."

For a brief instant, Moshe witnessed the Oberscharführer turn toward the commander with his jaw agape in surprise. Yet, the officer promptly regained composure, for even if he was dying with curiosity, he would never dare to question his superior.

Breitner turned and quietly addressed the officer. "Have them dress and take them to the washhouse and lock them inside. They are to have no contact with anyone; they should remain entirely isolated from the others, understood?"

"*Jawohl,* Herr Kommandant."

Breitner addressed the prisoners. "You will be confined to the washhouse," Breitner explained pointing in the direction of the large wooden barrack facing Block 11. "Where you will remain until"—Breitner dutifully consulted his watch—"let's say tomorrow morning, 0800. At that time you will inform me of your decision. You have fourteen hours to decide who, among you, will be executed. I am not interested in the criteria on which you base your decision: the youngest, the oldest, the most expendable, the least congenial . . in this manner, you are entirely free."

Breitner flashed a smile. The irony of his final directive had not escaped him.

"I ask only that tomorrow morning you give me a name. The others will then return to their blocks."

The prisoners knew that they were not, under any circumstances, to address the officers, let alone the commander in chief. Such an infraction signaled an irrevocable and immediate execution.

Breitner eyed each of the inmates one by one, relishing their disquietude. "Good. I hope I have made myself clear. Good night, *meine Herren!*"

He turned on his heels and in a most resolute military fashion, he began to make his way back to the office. After only a few steps, he stopped and turned to the men once more. His mouth bore a grin which Moshe instinctively feared. "Ah, I had nearly forgotten. If, by tomorrow morning, you fail to supply me with a name, all ten of you will be executed. Good luck to you."

The commander sat quietly in his study. The camp was dark. From the dormer windows, the night sky shrouded all but the faint silhouettes of the watchtowers. He interlaced his fingers, turned his palms outward, and extended his arms in a stretch, causing his joints to creak in submission. A soft knock was heard at the door.

"Yes?"

A little boy peered in from the doorway, standing not much taller than the handle itself. "Papa . . . can I come in?"

Breitner's face gave way to a smile.

"Why, of course, Felix! Come here!"

The little boy ran to his father, who without getting up, enveloped him in a warm embrace. The little boy smelled of soap. He was dressed in knee-length woolen trousers, a white dress shirt, and a little jacket complete with three small buttons down the front. On his feet, he wore a pair of lustrous little black lace-up shoes.

"Well, how was it today?"

"Herr Professor Kreutz did not come. He's not feeling well."

"You didn't have a lesson then?"

"Mum made me do some exercises and then I read a book."

"And which book was that?"

"A pirate book."

"Was it a good one?"

"Oh, it was really good. So many things happen. Papa, when I grow up, can I be a pirate?"

"Pirates are criminals, Felix."

"But in the story, they are good!"

"I'm not sure that's such a good idea."

"Do you think it's difficult to become a pirate? Do you have to take a test?"

"Well, first you'd have to learn to navigate the seas. If you like, you could enroll at the Naval Academy."

"Nooo!" Felix bore an expression of utter disgust. "They make you study there!"

"Well, my dear boy, we'll find something for you. In the meantime, I'd say you're still much too young for all of that. First things first, this summer I'll teach you how to swim."

"Felix, Felix, darling, where are you?" said a woman, her voice drifting into the study from the floor below.

Breitner and the little boy listened as the sound of footsteps traveled up the stairwell to the entrance of the study.

"Ah, there you are." Frieda stood in the doorway addressing the two. "Karl, darling, you finished early this evening."

"I made every effort to hurry home. I wanted to have dinner with you both." Breitner stood and greeted his wife with a kiss on the cheek.

"Well, then, I'll just go down to prepare. Come, Felix, let your father do his work."

"But, Mom, Papa wants to play a game of chess. He asked me,

didn't you, Papa?" The little boy turned to his father and gave him a wink.

"Yes, just for a quick game. . . ."

Frieda flashed an inquisitive glance toward her husband; usually he was not keen on having Felix underfoot while at work. Still, she left the two of them, closing the door behind her.

"And how did this happen?" Breitner commenced once the two were alone. "You don't usually like to play chess."

"I know, but you wanted to play, didn't you, Papa?"

The commander smiled softly. He opened up the chessboard and removed a few of the pieces. He placed them on the board as Felix quietly looked on.

"Papa, why are we not using all of the pieces?"

"Well, it's what you might call a variation of the game, you see." With that, he pointed to the principal pieces, one by one.

"But, Papa, the black king has only two knights, two bishops, a rook, and five pawns. And the whites have all of their pieces."

"It's not the entire game, Felix, my boy. It's the final round of a game. Not to worry, you can be the whites and I'll see what I can conjure up with these blacks."

"No, Papa. I want to play with the black pieces. Can I?"

"But the set is not complete. I don't think you can make much of it."

"That's okay, I like the black pieces. They look like pirates. And they're nicer, anyway."

"All right, my dear boy," sighed the commander. "Take the blacks if you so wish." He arranged their pieces accordingly.

And under his breath, he asked, "Let's see how this all plays out, shall we?"

1800 Hours

The barracks that served as the SS officers' washhouse was quite large, more like a Block. It had only one floor, which was constructed entirely of wood. And for the moment, they were its only inhabitants. The *Häfilnge* who had been assigned the task of the washing had returned to their barracks for the evening. The space carried with it a pervasive odor of detergent and lye. With timorous steps, the ten entered, studying their new surroundings. Many of them had never entered the washhouse before. At the far end of the room, a number of different appliances lined the wall: a steam cleaner, iron presses, and industrial-sized tubs for washing. A clothesline stretched across the center of the room, from which hung a dozen or so of the SS officer's uniforms. Blankets, jackets, civilian trousers, linens, and caps had been heaped into a pile near the entrance. A long table had been placed just inside the main door, flanked by wooden workbenches, which had been assembled within the compound's workshops. From high above, a barren lightbulb hung squarely over the table, casting a bleak light over the few objects in its labored reach. In a vain effort to quicken their pace, one of the SS officers shoved the inmate nearest him, a tall and rather gaunt boy, with the blunt end of his rifle. Inching farther away from the door, they moved along like a battered and abandoned flock.

The Oberscharführer released his grip on his rifle, allowing it to hang from its shoulder strap. From his pocket he removed a small stack of papers and a few pencils; items so rare that they had been all but inaccessible for Moshe within both Kanada and the offices at Buna.

"The commander ordered me to leave these with you; in the event that they are of service to you."

When none of the prisoners dared to come forward to receive the articles, the officer held open his hand and let the items fall loosely to the ground. Then, after a moment's contemplation, he knelt down and gathered the pieces into his hands once again. He stood before the prisoners and began, in a most methodical fashion, to shred each and every piece of paper until a myriad of confetti was strewn about the floor.

"Of course, he did not order me to give them to you in one piece!" He erupted into a fit of laughter.

With that, the SS officers exited the barracks, securing the door behind them. The inmates were alone again.

One of the ten began to walk about the large space, the sight of which they were not accustomed to. The others remained diffidently near the entrance, attempting to gain some sense of their new environment. Moshe knelt down and began to collect the scattered shreds of paper from off the floor. One by one, he carefully placed each scrap in his hand, taking great care not to crumple the remains.

"What's the matter, you need to wipe your Jewish ass or something?" a gruff German voice boomed.

Moshe turned to see Alexey, the aide to the *Blockältester,* towering over him. By virtue of his position within the hierarchy of the camp, he wore thick, heavy civilian clothes that were nothing like the cotton uniforms given to the other prisoners.

"I don't need these. Your tongue will do just fine."

At the barracks, such a situation would have elicited a series of sharp blows by way of Alexey and his club. Yet, in the anomalous and sudden circumstance, he knew not what to do. Any trace of the authority he once held in the barracks had vanished, placing Alexey at a very dangerous disadvantage. He took a few steps back, releasing a stream of grumbled expletives in Ukrainian from under his breath.

When Moshe had finished collecting every shred of paper, he placed them on the table under the sparse light. He laid them down one by one. He then shuffled them around, turning and repositioning each piece until they seemed to fit together. In a few short minutes, he had managed to reconstruct half a sheet of paper.

The tall gaunt boy, who was dressed in ill-fitting pants that barely covered his knees, made his way to the heap of clean laundry in the corner. His eyes glistened at the sight of such a profusion of goods.

Jan, the elderly Muslim, was reclining atop a stack of folded sheets and appeared to be sound asleep. Jacek, the head of their barrack, stood silently against the wall. Jiri, Elias, and Berkovitz timorously scanned the room, unsure of their own approach. The inmate branded as the Red Triangle, however, made his way to the table, so that he stood directly in front of Moshe.

"What's the matter, Otto, aren't you happy? Nine of us will be spared. Doesn't that seem like a rather good turnout?"

"Yes, but who?"

Moshe took a momentary leave from his efforts. In those few minutes that had passed, he had managed to construct one whole sheet of paper.

"We'll be the ones to decide; didn't you hear the Kommandant? Democracy through the eyes of a Nazi."

"I don't like this."

"Neither do I." Alexey approached the two men, appearing quite agitated. He towered over the men with his immense thick frame, his crooked nose, and his blackened teeth, and yet the circumstances had weakened him.

"What do you want?" Otto inquired, peering upward in a state of calm.

"To let you know that three men escaped from our barracks, and now we're the ones in trouble. All because of your friends, Otto."

"Just shut up. You don't know what you're talking about—"

"Don't I? The first was Grzegorz, you knew him quite well. Doesn't he run around with you?"

"He is a comrade and nothing more. I have many here at the camp. I bet you would like their names, wouldn't you, Alexey? And then you could play informant for the gestapo in exchange for an extra bowl of soup."

"Jesus, what a world!" Jiri suddenly exploded. The man who the others knew as the Pink Triangle was perched over a heap of blankets in the center of the sparsely lit room. His voice seemed to materialize from the air itself. "You would betray your fellow man for a bowl of *Wassersuppe*? Christ, I would have at least asked for a slice of bread!"

Alexey shrugged his shoulders. Pointing his finger at Otto, he continued, "You couldn't have *not* known about the escape. It's your fault that we're here."

Otto moved toward Alexey. He was at least half a foot shorter than Alexey, yet he was equally as stout. He had slaved in the harshest conditions, under some of the worst *Kommandos,* and never once did he utter even a whimper of complaint. He was respected throughout all of the KZ.

"I wouldn't say that if I were you. The resistance within the camp had nothing to do with it. It was a decision carried out by impulse; perhaps they simply knew when the opportune moment presented itself—"

"Or perhaps the German forces found them immediately; they executed them and then took the opportunity to entertain themselves at our expense."

Moshe's eyes remained fixed on the table; he continued to shuffle and sort through the scraps. He now had a second whole sheet of paper.

"Well." Otto nodded. "I suppose that theory cannot be ruled out entirely." His gaze then narrowed. "Watch yourself. Remember that no one here has forgotten that you've been the one who has beaten us every day. You and your boss—" He turned to Jacek, who had remained against the wall, somewhat guardedly. "But here, you hold no rank, you haven't your clubs or SS officers to protect you. If I have to choose someone to be executed, rest assured I've made my decision."

A heavy silence fell upon the room. Otto's avowal brought with it the reminder that they would be forced to select a name. And the time in which they had to choose was fleeting.

"Just as Cain shall not strike Abel," Elias spoke. He was seated atop a blanket; his eyes were closed. "I will not give a name. Ever. For God would not forgive such an act. Only He supplies us our destinies and dictates our fate."

"Well then, tell him now would be a good time to show up!" Jiri resounded from the far end of the room.

The boy, whose name no one knew, suddenly spoke. "When do you think they'll give us something to eat?"

"Do you think they're going to feed us?" Moshe replied, having finished reconstructing his third sheet of paper. "What do you think, Aristarchos?"

The Greek man responded with a violent stream of expletives in his own tongue.

"Do you know what they did to one poor fellow? He needed his appendix removed, so they took him to Ka-Be, where they placed him under anesthesia, carried out the operation without complication, and then granted him fifteen days to recuperate. And when he had fully recovered, they ordered him to be sent to the *kremchy*. It would be no small wonder if they brought us salmon and caviar tonight, only to execute every last one of us tomorrow."

"They intend to kill only one of us," Otto interjected. "What do you think they aim to do?"

"It's that *Kommandant!*" This was followed by more swearing from Aristarchos. "Did you not see him? He's bored and entertains himself by way of these little games. If it were up to me . . ." He lapsed into Greek; his aggravated retort was understood only by Moshe, who broke into a smile.

Berkovitz, who had been standing near the entrance, suddenly commenced, "We mustn't get worked up. They could come for us tonight even."

"Is that what you're hoping for?" Otto inquired curtly.

"No, I only mean that . . . it's not over just yet."

"For nine of us it certainly isn't," Moshe interjected. Then, having reconsidered: "No, nothing is for certain."

"But that's just it, you see, I have to ask myself, why exactly were we chosen?" Berkovitz began. "Personally, I hardly know Grzegorz. And as for the others, I've never even spoken to them."

"What's your point?"

"And even you, Moshe. You knew Grzegorz, but I wouldn't go so far as to say that he was your friend."

"He bought something from me once. But I can't say he ever invited me to his house for tea and cake."

"But the same can be said, more or less, for each of us here. It seems as if the Germans simply chose at random. It's as if they shuffled the deck, closed their eyes, and pulled the cards."

"I doubt that," Jacek, the head of the barrack, interjected while still seeking refuge against the wall. They were the first words he had spoken since arriving at the washhouse. "It isn't in their nature."

"You mean in *yours*," Otto retorted menacingly.

"You're right," Moshe intervened "Their every decision is ruled by precision and efficiency. They could not have simply chosen us at random."

"They needed ten hostages and here we are. They took the first ten names in their registry."

"They had *our* numbers. That couldn't have been the case."

"My thought is that perhaps someone, not everyone, but someone here knew of the escape. And they said nothing." Jacek had a mellifluous voice that bore a static drone. And yet, his accusation stung nonetheless, and for a moment, the room quieted.

"And why would anyone need to hide it?" The gangly young man broke the silence as he took a seat.

"Because that individual would be held responsible for our current predicament, and we would in turn willingly have him executed," responded Otto.

"And one mustn't exclude the notion that maybe this person aims to carry out his own escape. Perhaps the jackboots never did find the route the prisoners used to flee. And maybe this person intends to make his exit the same way" Moshe's gaze remained resolutely fixed on the table. Each of the ten *Häftlinge* glanced around the room, asking themselves who might be privy to such information. And if he would take them along.

Jiri's voice broke the nervous silence that had fallen upon the barrack. They all looked up in shock, for the Pink Triangle had suddenly thrown aside two Nazi uniforms that hung from the clothesline on either side of him, creating what looked like an impromptu stage.

"*In dem Schatten dunkler Lauben . . .*"

He sang with an effeminate timbre, yet he was decisively in tune. The others looked on, bewildered by the stark contrast of the song and the situation that they now faced.

Each day, just before the work Kommandos entered and left, the camp's orchestra could be heard playing different melodies, all of which were either military marches or, at best, *Rosamunde*. Jiri, however, was in the midst of a song that no one ever dreamed would be heard in a KZ.

Little by little, the Pink Triangle made his way into the light cast by the barren bulb. There was a sinuous elegance to his movements, a cross between a walk and a dance step, like a ballerina entering to take her place on stage. His body moved and shifted the way a woman's might in high heels. His feet slid forward across the floor as if he were on ice. His shoulders were back, his head straight; even his striped uniform seemed to have transformed into a sort of evening gown.

"*Sassen beide Hand in Hand . . .*"

He passed through the others, making his way to the center of the room and bearing a most suggestive smile. Moshe realized then that Jiri was anything but a Muslim. His body, though thin, was not emaciated like the others. It was clear that he had been the frequent recipient of gifts in exchange for sexual favors carried out on the many *Prominenten*.

"*Sass ein Jäger mit seiner Lola . . .*"

Otto made an aggravated grimace.

Jiri sashayed his way to the table where he then spun around and took a seat in a most provocative manner. He held two of his fingers to his lips, as if clasping a cigarette, and blew an imaginary stream of smoke into the air.

"Hello, beautiful," he whispered to Alexey. Yet, when he reached across to caress the face of the barrack leader's aide, Alexey thrust aside Jiri's arm so violently that he tumbled to the floor. Alexey was now in a state of fury, one which the other prisoners had learned to fear. He grabbed one of the chairs and hurled it across the room. Jiri recoiled in pain on the floor. Alexey had lost control. With two heavy strides, he now hovered over Jiri and prepared to unleash his fury with his boot.

"*Stop!*"

Jacek interceded without ever leaving his post.

"Stop."

Alexey looked up with a blurred fury, and for a moment, Moshe thought he might throw himself upon the *Blockältester*. Yet the rage that had so suddenly seized him seemed to dissipate with the same velocity. He stood motionless, his lungs heaving. It was clear that it must have taken a tremendous effort to maintain his restraint. Yet they had seen it happen other times too, his violence kept in check by a disapproving glance from the barrack leader.

Otto leaned over to help Jiri, who whimpered tremulously on the floor.

"Come on now, get up. He didn't hurt you."

He offered his hand but Jiri fiercely refused it.

"Go away! Even you . . . you're just like all the others."

"What does that mean?"

"Oh, really! You know full well that at the end of all of this you're going to have to give one name to the commander, and it's going to be mine!"

"You don't know what you're talking about. I think the lack of food has gone to your head."

"Don't act as if this comes as a surprise." Jiri's apparent fragility had mutated into a sudden cold rage. "Even you, with your seemingly unwavering duty as the people's guardian, you detest me; you have nothing but contempt for me. Isn't that so? For two thousand years, you have persecuted people like me . . . and now that you have me, you're going to hand me off to the Kommandant. So I can be your sacrificial angel." The same sorrowful sadness shrouded the room once again. "But don't worry, I understand. And even now, I forgive you."

Moshe facetiously applauded the tirade.

"Bravo, Jiri. But the box office is closed. They didn't sell a single ticket to the show; I'm afraid your little *Kabarett* piece is going to have to go on hiatus for a while. You might save your performance for next season."

His biting words left Jiri quite cross. Forgetting the pain he had so vehemently lamented a short while ago, he sprung from the floor. He headed to one of the darker corners of the room with quick agitated steps, sweeping through the middle of the same two dangling uniforms with a brush of his arms.

Meanwhile, Jacek had removed himself from the ordeal and was perusing the washhouse, scouring each and every corner. He lifted every pile of linens and clothing, passing his hand under each one. His search seemed a very methodical undertaking. Moshe watched from the other side of the room, shaking his head.

Jacek had inspected nearly half of the immense room when the others heard him shout, "Aha!"

He returned to the table; under the bleak light of the bulb the *Häftlinge* could make out what he held in his hand: a black, moldy, half-eaten piece of bread.

"I knew that someone would have hidden a piece of something somewhere. There's always some amateur who thinks he's crafty by hiding away his own supply. I bet he ended up in the crematorium before he ever had a chance to stash it."

Just the sight of it was enough to aggravate the sharp pang of hunger they each endured without end. But no one approached Jacek.

From his pocket, the barrack leader withdrew a spoon with a sharp handle that doubled as a knife. He placed the bread on the table. Nine pairs of eyes ravenously followed his every move. Just as he began to cut a slice, a voice shouted in defiance.

"Stop!"

Jacek looked up, accosted by Otto's menacing stare. Alexey loomed ominously, ready to intervene.

"Leave the bread where it is," Otto's voice carried neither fear nor uncertainty; he spoke with clear and resolute authority. "Leave it."

Jacek turned with a sidelong smile. "And why should I?"

"We're no longer in the barrack, and you're no longer the *Blockältester*. The SS officers won't come to your aid. You're on your own. Just like the rest of us here. That bread will be divided among all of us."

A sudden jolt of pain tore through each of their stomachs. Even if dividing the bread into ten pieces meant the rations would be minuscule, it was still better than nothing; moreover, it had come without the weight of anticipation.

"But I was the one to find it. It does belong to me then, doesn't it?"

"Hardly. We're no longer under Nazi rule here. Tonight we are on equal footing. If anything, we are more obligated than ever to extend our good graces to one another, in order to ensure that, come tomorrow, we are not beaten or burned to death. Here, tonight, we have the opportunity to be civil to one another once again, to be equals. And so, that bread will be shared."

Alexey lingered nearby, audibly grinding his teeth, ready to fight. Jacek stood, silently assessing the situation.

After a few, seemingly interminable seconds, Jacek raised his arm in the direction of Alexey, much in the same way one might restrain a ferocious dog.

"All right then. One piece of bread divided into the ten portions will do little to alleviate your hunger. But if that's what you want."

Otto approached the table. Retrieving Jacek's spoon, he took the sharp-handled end and with a surgeon's precision, he began to slice the bread into ten identical portions. The ten slices lay on the table; dry and with a greenish hue, and yet, irresistibly inviting.

"Move back," Otto ordered; the others obeyed. Moshe stood and moved to the far end of the room. Alexey, after having been forced to restrain his rage, turned away too.

The Red had changed the order of the food distribution.

"Elias?" Otto petitioned.

"Three," he answered, without looking up. He then approached the table. Otto handed him the third slice of bread.

"Jiri."

"Ten."

The Pink Triangle, by now somewhat recovered, took his piece.

"Berkovitz . . . Aristarchos . . . Jacek . . . Alexey . . . eh, and you . . . what's your name?"

The boy, so proselytized by the process, answered only, "Five."

"Moshe."

"Zero."

A silence shrouded in uncertainty fell about the room.

"Moshe—"

"Zero, I said. I don't want any of that bread. It's assuredly infested with lice or some other putrid atrocity of the like."

"Moshe! We have no assurance that they'll bring us anything at all to eat. I . . ."

Moshe leaned against the table.

"Fine then, give it here."

He blindly plucked one of the slices from off of the table. He crossed the room to Jan, who lay motionless atop the folded sheets on the floor.

Offering him the piece Moshe explained, "This bread is rancid . . . and I don't care to eat. I'm accustomed to better."

The old man peered at the morsel of food with a vacuous stare, confused by the exchange. And then suddenly, his eyes gave way to a lucid glimmer.

"I thank you, but I no longer need it."

"Jan, that's rubbish. I—"

"Now, listen to me. I am an old man at death's door. I've not the strength to keep up this fight. I have not the will to carry on. Do you understand what I'm saying? That bread would be wasted on me." With that, he was overcome by a convulsive fit of coughing.

"Listen, I don't care whether you do or don't have the will to carry on, but you need to eat the bread. Would you rather I give it to Jacek?"

The tired old man shook his head, to which Moshe responded with a near smile.

"All right then."

Jan conceded and just as he prepared to bite into his grievous morsel, Otto intervened.

"If you want to deny yourself your ration, Moshe, that's quite all right. But it ought to be redistributed to everyone here. You forfeit your rights, and it now will go back to the collective group."

"Otto, don't be ridiculous. If you were to divide it yet again into nine scant pieces, there would not be enough of a crumb to satisfy a mouse. For once, try to employ a bit of reason without theorizing what the Communist Party would do."

Moshe returned his focus to the scraps of paper still in pieces on the table.

The bread had been distributed. Everyone had received their due portion. Some chose to savor each morsel of their slice, while others devoured it in a few swift, determined bites. Regardless of their approach, within a few seconds, all the divvied portions had been consumed.

"There's still a crumb over here on the table," Moshe observed. "Would you like to divide it up as well, Otto?"

The Red Triangle ignored his provocations, and instead, turned to address Jacek.

"You were the one that found the bread, whatever is left is rightfully yours."

Jacek seemed confounded for a moment, and then crossed to the table. He swept the surface of the wooden surface with the side of his hand, catching the crumbs in his palm. He then tilted his head and inhaled the last few scant crumbs under the covetous watch of the others.

"Would that be a production-based reward bestowed by your *kolkhoz*?" Moshe asked, but Otto only shrugged.

Berkovitz shuffled his feet as he paced around the table, every now and then stopping to lift his glasses and rub the bridge of his nose. He was a man accustomed to answering only to himself. Even within the confines of camp, thanks to his intelligence and his innumerable connections, he was able to maintain that freedom to some extent. Yet, there in the washhouse, he was at the utter mercy of all the others. Rounding the table near Moshe, he stopped and pointed in the direction of the many fragments of paper.

"What are you doing?"

"Putting these sheets back together."

"Why?"

Moshe shrugged.

"I don't know. Perhaps it's because I have nothing else to do. Perhaps it's because I don't want to grant them any sort of victory. Or maybe I . . ."

He paused for a brief second to situate two last scraps. He had managed to reconstruct each and every one of the sheets, which now lay across the table, covering nearly all of its surface.

"I like puzzles. They've always intrigued me. I know *Herr Kommandant* enjoys his chess, but I've never been much for it. The black-and-white-checked board gives me a headache. Though it's hardly surprising that a German would fancy such a concept. As for me, I prefer puzzles. I once bought a five-thousand-piece puzzle; it was from Russia and it was utterly exquisite."

"I can't say I've ever attempted one."

"You were too busy making money, Berkovitz. Tell the truth now, have you ever tasted the sweetness of idle pleasures? Have you ever just spent a few hours of your time devoted to something that you knew would amount to nothing?"

Berkovitz's hand skimmed over the now uniform scraps that lay upon the table.

"You see?" Moshe continued, "Puzzles require an eye for detail. At first, the colors serve as your guide. Then, you begin to spot the lines and curves of each shape. You see, you must be able to distinguish even the most microscopic differences, yet you must never lose sight of the greater picture either, for you'll find yourself in trouble if you focus only on the particulars. You must always keep all perspectives in your line of sight, both the big and the small. In that way, you learn to immerse yourself in two completely separate planes of thought."

"Don't pay him any mind!" Elias barked, his face flushed in aggravation. "He talks only to confuse you. He'll say one thing and ten minutes later, just the opposite!"

"All right, enough!" Alexey exploded from the opposite end of the table, slamming his hand against the wooden surface and sending the scraps, which had been so painstakingly configured, flying once more through the air. "I've had it with your stupid conversations!"

Moshe recoiled in an attempt to avoid any contact with Alexey's fist. He watched as the pieces fluttered to the ground; he then knelt with utter calm and began, once again, to pick up the pieces.

Alexey, enraged by the lack of reaction, let out a volley of expletives.

From the pallet on the floor where Jan now lay, the others could hear him as he broke into another convulsive fit of coughs. His body had deteriorated to a heap of bones covered in a thin, fragile film of dry and wrinkled skin that shook with each cough, as if being accosted by detonations from within. Each of the other nine cast their glances away, petrified by the idea of incumbent death.

Jan was still struggling when the door to the barrack flung open. The Oberscharführer, who had first accompanied them to the barracks offering only torn shreds of paper, stood at the entrance. The impudent air he bore during his first visit had been replaced by a hurried state of duty.

"*Aufstehen!*"

All but Jan, who still fought to control his convulsions, sprang to their feet and turned to face the SS officer. The sight of the officer both alarmed and tormented the prisoners. *What was happening? Had the commander retracted his decision and now intended to execute all ten hostages? Or had they managed to catch the runaways?* The officer could sense the mental anguish that his presence had caused, and he relished their visible disquietude. After a moment's torment, he pulled a sheet of paper, which had been tucked away in his pocket, and under the bleak light, read aloud what would suffice as the only explanation for his visit.

"190.826 . . . 116.125 . . . this way! Now!"

The tall and somewhat gaunt prisoner stood stock-still, yet his expression gave way to the utter terror that consumed him. Aristarchos, however, quietly took a step forward without protest.

The officer motioned toward the exit.

"Move. This way! *Los!*"

The young gangly man and his elderly Greek counterpart made their way to the door. There was no farewell; their exit allowed only time enough for Aristarchos to cast a subtle glance in Moshe's direction. The door then closed, and the remaining eight captives were left alone once again, each silently questioning what was to come.

"What's wrong Papa? What are you doing?"

Felix, perplexed, watched as his father pulled two black pawns from the board. He held them in his hand for a moment, lost in thought.

"What are you thinking about, Papa?"

"I'm afraid I've set the game up quite poorly. There are too many pawns. I had hoped for a more challenging match, you see."

Breitner placed the two pawns on the desk and surveyed the other pieces in the chess box. He studied the board for a moment and then, with a calm repose, he pulled out two new pieces and placed them on the board.

"You gave me a rook and a queen. Are you sure, Papa?"

Breitner moved momentarily away from the board and crossed to the window that gave way to a view that encompassed the whole of the camp. He smiled with contentment.

"Yes, I think so. It should prove to be a most interesting game."

1900 Hours

"Where are they taking them?"

Jiri paced back and forth in front of the door, unable to control his frenzied perturbation. "Back to the barracks? Or the bunker, maybe? Or—"

"Will they be executed?" Moshe interjected on his behalf. "First of all, we don't know. And second, we didn't hear any shots fired. And lastly, we're the ones who are still here. Our situation has yet to change. It's useless to continue on with these presupposed conceits."

"Do you hear that, my friends? We have a new prophet among us," Elias interceded.

Berkovitz, too, seemed irritated by the continual rhetoric.

"Yes, but why did they choose them? Did anyone know the boy?"

The others shook their heads.

"He arrived just a few days ago," Jacek explained. "I think he's a Slovak, or something of the sort, but he's doesn't say very much. He's young, only eighteen or nineteen."

"And what about Aristrachos?" Jiri implored. "He's an old

man. Everyone here has such a high regard for him, even the SS officers. He's been nothing but a hard worker."

"Maybe they wanted to be sure his life was spared," Jacek contended and raised his shoulders.

"And the boy did seem to be in rather good health," Berkovitz remarked.

"Perhaps they have a *prominent* who protects them," Jiri carried on.

"Or perhaps they were just spies," Otto muttered from beneath his scowl.

"The boy never said a word to anyone. We don't even know his name. Isn't that a little odd?" Jiri said.

"There has been no talk of a convoy arriving from Slovakia in the last few days. Can you attest to that, Jacek?" Otto asked.

Jacek gave a nod.

Otto's grimace deepened.

"Jiri, you're asking a thief to count your money. Don't you get it? It's in Jacek's every interest to persuade you that the boy was a spy. That way, you'll never suspect him."

"Shut up!" Alexey roared.

"And if I don't? What then? You'll call the *Lagerältester* to come and beat me?"

Alexey seethed with an anger so fractious that no words came forth, nor did he allow his retort to come by way of his fist, which was usually his preferred means. Yet, the situation now presented irrefutably different boundaries. Were he to attack Otto—who, as it were, had no difficulty defending himself— one of the other inmates would undoubtedly intervene. Not Jiri, of course, and neither Jan nor Elias. But perhaps Berkovitz. Or even Moshe.

Jacek said, "Think for a minute. If Alexey or I were spies, would we have ended up in here?"

"The SS might have thought it advantageous to mix you in with all of us; maybe you'd discover something they hadn't."

Elias, who had been following the conversation from the far corner of the room, inched closer with the same solemn demeanor that he perpetually bore.

" 'Then, let me die with the Philistines,' so it was that Samson pleaded in the Temple of Dagon. Is this also what you want? For the fall of one man to wreak havoc upon the rest of us? Let us be brothers. For only if we are united will we prevail against our enemies."

"Elias, this isn't the synagogue. No one wants to hear your sermon," Alexey snapped contemptuously; he scrambled to his feet and stood, looming over the others. "Enough of this. The commander ordered that we choose someone to be executed. So let's get on with it. The sooner we decide, the sooner it will all be over."

"You're in quite the hurry," Moshe said. "Another engagement, I imagine?"

"Oh, but of course." Jiri swished, quick to follow suit. "You have some *pipel* waiting for you in the barracks? I'm no good anymore?"

Jiri's retort was met by a sharp and dismissive shove from Alexey.

Unharmed, Jiri continued with a sigh. "Poor little me! Why is it that I always fall for the bad ones?"

"Enough! Let's go!" Alexey thundered.

"Jiri's right," Moshe said. "What's the hurry? Let's just wait. Maybe something will change course; the commander might retract the order, or maybe an English air raid will come and bomb the whole place—"

"No!"

In that instant, each and every one of the prisoners turned

toward Otto. The man branded the Red repeated, "You're all wrong. We need to do this now."

The eight looked on in bewilderment. Otto rose to his feet and began to pace methodically back and forth in front of the nearby window that looked out onto the deserted dark camp. No one was permitted outside of the barracks after the bells tolled; if they were, they would face immediate execution. Otto stopped.

"Alexey's right. We need to make our decision now. If we wait any longer, the commander could retract his proposal and execute all of us. We have the chance to save seven of us here; we mustn't waste it." Otto's rhetoric ceased and he turned once again to the floor, taking two or three paces at a time before coming to a halt, only to carry on the pattern once again. Unable to gain control of his nerves, the uneven sequence of steps seemed to pacify him somewhat. Moshe watched, perplexed.

"All right then, let's go ahead. Otto, for example, who would you choose?"

Otto commenced his response without breaking his awkward gait. "For me, there is no distinction; there exists neither Jews, nor Christians, nor Buddhists, nor anything of the sort. For me, there exists only those who exploit and those who are exploited. Even among the Jews these two categories exist. Elias, for example, you are the exploited."

Elias did not answer.

"You worked in insurance, if I'm not mistaken."

"In Warsaw. I was the legal head of the office."

"And what happened when the Nazis arrived?"

"They revoked all of my responsibilities. At first, they permitted me to do some of the more subordinate tasks; I went from house to house to collect insurance claims. After a while that no longer sufficed; I was informed that it irritated the clients to have to speak directly with a Jew. In the end, the only position allotted to me was that of janitor."

"And you did it?"

"I was respecting God's will. Often, He tests us, and those who must endure the greatest of trials are often His most beloved."

"Good, then I'm safe!" Jiri sneered. "I can't imagine I'm one of his favorites."

"And so the legal head of the office is reduced to sweeping floors," Otto reprised. "And what of your colleagues?"

"There was one, unbeknown to the rest, who unfailingly offered words of encouragement. The others however, seemed intent on magnifying my degraded state. They would call me in after having defecated on the floor, forcing me to clean their filth and refuse on my hands and knees. And once, while kneeling to scrub the floor, my former colleague stood over me . . . and urinated . . . and then he . . ."

The rabbi fell silent.

"And then he what?" Otto implored.

"And then he called the others over. They stripped me naked . . . and called me a dirty Jew . . . they accused me of being unclean . . . they bashed my head into the floor . . . they threw me into . . . into the . . ."

Elias's voice trembled and then weakly trailed off into silence once more; so overcome was he by the memory, he had not the will to continue.

Otto looked at the others.

"Well, then? Would you choose Elias?"

"A moment ago, you said that there were Jews who exploited others. Who were you thinking of?" Jiri demanded inquisitively.

"Of him." Otto pointed in the direction of Berkovitz. "He didn't simply work at an insurance company like Elias, he ran one. His rank was one of great esteem; one that permitted him to move and manipulate mountains of money. His career was built on what he could create and destroy. He could throw hundreds of families out on the street with a wag of his little finger."

"Far from the truth!" Berkovitz countered in a voice that conveyed both composure and imperturbable conviction. He was accustomed to arbitrating contentions within the administrative councils. "If anything, in my line of work I had the privilege of creating thousands of job opportunities. And in turn, those thousands of families could put food on their tables."

"Well now, the jackboots must have not been terribly impressed with your efforts, isn't that so?" Moshe said.

Berkovitz lifted his glasses from the bridge of his nose and rubbed his eyelids.

"I remember when Robert Flick, from Industrie-Maschinen AG, came to see me one day. Even with the war commissions, the company was doing poorly. The shareholders had squandered a vast sum of their earnings on women, cars, and gambling. He had come to request a loan of a most incomprehensible amount; he wanted two million. Of all people, he came to me. He was part of one of the most exclusive circles in the Fascist Party; he could have just as easily gone to the Reichsführer for any sum of money he wanted! And yet, he came to me, a Jew, and asked for money."

"I bet you felt like God himself at that very moment."

"Perhaps I did. And perhaps, as a result, it clouded my judgment. I don't deny that. Flick informed me that, in exchange, he would try to help me and my family in some way. He told me that the Reich sought to cleanse the whole of Germany by removing all Judaic presence, but that not all Jews were considered deleterious. There were those who were still considered to be of use in servicing *Großdeutschland*. And the party, in turn, would never overlook the efforts of such individuals."

"And you believed him?"

"Yes, I believed him. I saw to it that the bank approved his loan. When I called him with the news, I was permitted only a brief exchange with his secretary. They came for me the morning after, arriving at dawn. Fortunately, I had already arranged for my wife and child to seek refuge elsewhere. They forced me out of my home just as they found me; wearing only pajamas, a housecoat, and my slippers. They loaded me into a car, and they delivered me to the chief SS commander. As they dragged me from my home, I remember catching sight of a car parked along the road. It was a dark Mercedes. One that I recognized. In the backseat sat Robert Flick. As we passed him, he rolled down his window and watched me. I'm sure of it. He had come all that way just to enjoy the show. He cast a disparaging glance in my direction, then the Mercedes started up and sped away."

"I've just a remembered an old Yiddish joke. Anyone want to hear it?" Jiri offered.

"No," Moshe declined.

"Fine, have it your way." After a moment's repose, Jiri began, "Two rabbis travel to Rome. While there, they see a sign in front of a church that reads: 'Two thousand lire offered to whoever converts to Catholicism.' The two men are naturally shocked and offended. One says to the other, 'I'm going to see if there's any truth to this.' A few minutes pass and the rabbi exits the church. The other then asks, 'So? Is it true that they're giving away two thousand lire if you're willing to convert?' The other smirks and says: 'Two thousand lire? Money really is all you Jews think about!'"

Only Moshe laughed. Berkovitz remained imperturbable. And Otto was not one for jokes.

"You simply got what you deserved," the Red spouted. "The money that you gave to those jackboots was money that was stolen from the working class, from those who lived and suffered in squalid makeshift holes without light or air, while you, I can only imagine, lorded over a splendid villa with a butler and a pool—"

"What's this? A lecture in social politics?" Moshe protested.

"It's the simple truth. There are those who exploit and those who are exploited. Some have chosen the path to religious enlightenment, like Elias. Some have chosen to renounce the system, like myself. And some have chosen to aid in the efforts of those who exploit. Would you not agree, Alexey?"

"Scheiße!"

"Yes, and the expletives are only fitting. No one has forgotten that you were the one to beat us, to attack us in our weakest moments, when we were exhausted and broken from labor. No one has forgotten your boot smashing against us so that you might receive an approving nod from the SS officers. You even helped them, willingly, when they forced a group of Jews to line up along the stairs, each holding a heavy boulder on their backs, only to shoot and kill the man on the highest step so that he tumbled downward and helplessly dragged the others in his wake. You laughed, Alexey, *you laughed!*"

A silence fell upon the room. Most of them had a vivid recollection of that day despite having fought to obliterate the scene from their memory.

Alexey leaned back and let his shoulders fall against the wall. Even if equipped only with animal instinct, he understood that things looked grim.

"Don't test me. Don't test me or it will end badly for all of you."

"Wait a moment, my brothers," Elias spoke. "Let not our actions be dictated by rage. Do any of you remember the story of Gideon of Ofra?"

"No, but I have a feeling you'll enlighten us."

"Gideon brought peace to two warring tribes of Israel; they

then united to fight against and overthrow their common enemy, the Midianites. He sent word by way of messengers to the tribes of the Mannaseh, Asher, Zebulon, and Naphtali, and together they marched to defeat their enemies."

"And it was a bloody and savage defeat if I recall," Moshe added under his breath.

"Quiet!" Elias barked, though the situation hardly seemed to merit such a brusque response. "And we must do the same: we must unite against the enemy. Even if our tribes, until now, have fostered nothing but distrust for one another; now is the moment for us to join together."

Otto scoffed. Religious drivel agitated him.

"And what do you say to all of this, Jiri?"

"A Russian writer once said, 'An ally has to be watched just like an enemy.' "

"*Enough!* Stop all of this, you dirty, disgusting Jews. I won't be the one taken to the commandant!" Alexey, with his back to the wall, pulled something from his pocket. It was a knife, long and slender; it looked crudely forged and had likely been melded in one of the many clandestine annexes within the camp.

"You won't give them my name. If you do, I'll kill you all, one by one."

The others froze. Moshe carefully followed the crude weapon that Alexey now held, which threatened a murderous end for any one of them. Even if they were to join together, they would not be able to overpower the *Blockältester's* aide. And someone would lose their life because of it. And besides, who would have been willing to fight? Not Elias nor Jan, the eldest of the group. Not Jiri, and assuredly not Jacek. In truth, Jacek would have probably fought alongside their enemy.

"Nor him." Alexey held out his knife, pointing in the direction of Jacek. "He won't be chosen either."

"But look," Moshe said. "What moving loyalty to his master." Moshe paused. "Or perhaps, you fear that if Jacek were to be executed, his replacement might choose another henchman? And then you'd be back among us poor *Häftlinge,* who might not be so readily welcoming . . ."

The situation had become a stalemate. No one dared move. Alexey waved the knife through the air, yet in the absence of aggression, the gesture seemed hollow and to some extent absurd.

Jacek spoke, shattering what seemed an impenetrable silence.

"Put the knife away, Alexey."

"But—"

"What's the use? Who are you trying to fight? Jan, Jiri, Elias? And for what? Put it away."

Jiri, who had been standing at the opposite end of the table, inched his way closer to Jacek.

"Huh . . . but didn't you . . ."

Jiri grabbed hold of the cord from which the lightbulb dangled, and steered it toward Jacek so that the light shone on his face.

"Leave the lightbulb where it is!" Otto clamored with such intensity that the others fell silent once again. Having realized the effect of his outburst, he lowered his tone. "Be careful, those wires are exposed. You could get shocked," he said.

Jiri took no notice and rounded the table toward Jacek. He stopped directly in front of him.

"Yes, I know you."

Jacek made no effort to evade his stare. He stood, cold and impassive, just as before.

"Yes, I do believe I know you as well!" Moshe said.

"No, I mean to say . . . outside of the camp."

Jiri had caught the attention of the others. Even Elias seemed intrigued by his sudden revelation.

"I saw you play."

Jacek gave no reaction.

"You were stupendous. With that sweat-soaked jersey that clung to your chest—"

"You can leave out the maudlin details and just tell us the rest," prompted Moshe.

Jiri turned toward his newly collected audience, one that he was quite content to have.

"Jacek was a footballer. A really brilliant one, I'm quite certain. Well, not entirely certain since I know nothing about the game. But, I liked going to the stadium to see those handsome boys play."

"Is that true?"

Jacek gave a nod.

"I played in first division with Ruch Chorzów. I was a central defender. I played a few good games. Then . . . the war came."

"A defender . . . so that's how it is that you're so very good at keeping watch," Moshe said.

"But that's all over now," Jacek continued, "Even if I managed to leave here, I'd be too old to play."

"Please, don't make me cry, I'm quite tenderhearted."

"You're right, Moshe. If we want a chance at survival, there's no point in wallowing in the past. We must focus on the present."

"Yes, correct. Now, what would you say to choosing Alexey? Frankly, I think it's more than fair."

"We could," Jacek replied, "but then again, we don't have to." He paused. "Why not choose Otto instead?"

"Otto? And why would we do that?" Berkovitz asked. "He's done no harm to anyone."

"Are you sure of that? The escape was organized by his comrades, there's no doubt of that. And it's the very reason that we're all here. Don't you understand? We're just meat on a butcher block and nothing more. For him, there is only the resistance, and anyone is worth sacrificing for the sake of those ideals."

Everyone turned toward the man who had been labeled the Red Triangle.

"Otto, what do you say? Jacek is right, isn't he?"

"The resistance is occupying key posts within the camp, aren't any of you aware of this?" Jacek droned on in a voice that seemed ever unchanging. "But you Jews could not care any less. The only thing that seems of any importance to you is clearing the way for the arrival of the Russians. You'd better hope no Muslims intervene."

"That's hardly the truth. The resistance is concerned for everyone's well-being. Its objective is to help and protect the people. One must never lose sight of the collective good."

"And I'd bet that you're part of this collective good, am I right?" Moshe asked.

"Wait, there's something else . . ." said Jacek.

The inmates held their breath.

"Otto is *German*."

He spoke with the same fury and contempt as the others had. It was true that, though Otto was a *Häftling* who lived, slept, and ate with all the other prisoners, there was an intangible and indisputable separation between himself and the others. He was German. It was difficult to forget something of that nature.

"I'm telling you—" Jacek began again but his explanation suddenly halted, for there was a noise just outside the barrack.

The door opened. Again all but Jan scrambled to their feet.

"Well? Have you come to a decision?"

The Oberscharführer entered the washhouse. He eyed the inmates, one by one, then his gaze settled on the scraps of white paper atop the table.

"Not yet? You better hurry. *Schnell!* You heard the orders of *Herr Kommandant*. If you have not made a decision by tomorrow morning, he will meet all of you at the execution wall. As soon as you come to a decision, open the doors. We'll be outside."

The warrant officer turned on his heels and directed his attention to someone just outside of the entryway.

"*Herein!*" he shouted.

A shadow of a long and slender figure appeared in the doorway. It halted for a moment on the threshold, then the figure entered the room.

It was a new prisoner. His hair was longer than that of the others, and though it hardly reached a centimeter in length, one could see that he was blond. His cheekbones were quite prominent and his nose was angular. He wore civilian clothes that bore little evidence of much wear and a thick leather jacket with a fur-lined collar. On his feet were a pair of lustrous leather shoes. His hands were not blistered from the cold or calloused from endless hours of labor, and his body showed no sign of weakness.

The warrant officer exited and closed the door behind him.

The new detainee looked around him; the other eight eyed him warily.

"What's your name?" Alexey asked gruffly.

"Paul."

"Paul or Paula?"

He offered no response. Instead, he crossed the room under the watchful eyes of the others and stood against the opposite wall.

Alexey tailed behind him.

"Say who you are. We need to know what you do and why you're here."

"And all of you?"

"We already know one another."

"Well, you ought to be a little more patient then."

"All right, move along, Alexey," Moshe said. "Can't you see you're making our guest uncomfortable?" He stood up from the table and crossed the room to the new arrival.

With his arms open wide, Moshe began, "You have to forgive him. The mood here at the camp has ruined him. Do you know the reason that we're all here?"

"The prophet . . . Here he goes again!" Elias quietly muttered out of earshot from the others.

"You tell me."

"Three *Häftlinge* escaped. The commandant ordered that ten prisoners be killed in their place. But at the last minute, he changed his mind and has ruled that one should be executed. And so you see . . ." He paused. "It is up to us to decide who that will be. So, it's best that you introduce yourself."

Otto, who seemed wholly uninterested in the matter, continued pacing back and forth, never breaking his awkward pattern. Jiri, instead, crossed the room with willowy steps to where the new prisoner now stood. He studied the blond man for a moment and then stretched out his hand as if reaching to touch the man's chest. With only a few inches between them, he suddenly stopped.

"Quite the body," he commented. "It's not often you find this in the KZ."

"True," Moshe said suspiciously. "Seems as though you've had more than enough to eat. Have you just arrived?"

"There've been no trains for days now," Jacek remarked flatly. "Not a one."

Paul remained silent. His expression gave way to neither relief nor fear, making him altogether indecipherable.

Berkovitz made his way over as well.

"All right, come on, tell us everything. It's better for you, don't you understand? In here, we need to know everything. We need to be able to weigh out the good and the bad."

"In order to choose?" Paul asked.

"Yes, in order to choose," Moshe replied. "You see, we—" He stopped short. Something had caught his attention from the corner of his eye. He turned toward Otto. The Red took notice and for a moment halted his endless uneven pacing.

"What is it?" he demanded coarsely.

Moshe gave no answer, but watched him with a sudden intensity.

"We must make a decision." Otto changed the subject. "How should we begin?"

"Haste is often the workings of the devil," Elias spoke. "Do you remember the story of Ezekiel as it was written in the Talmud?"

Jiri cast his eyes toward the ceiling and whispered to Berkovitz, "Here we go again . . ."

"Ezekiel found himself at war with Sennacherib. He knew not what to do. And so, he invoked the Almighty and said to Him, 'I cannot pursue my enemy just as I cannot defend myself against him; I pray only that you smite him, O charitable one, whilst I sleep . . .'"

"Are you saying that we stretch out here on these sheets and have a nap?" Jacek asked.

"I am saying that we must pray to God so that He may show us the way. Often, a decision made in haste is one to be later repented. And sometimes, as you know, knots can untangle all by themselves."

Moshe turned to the others. "Well, what do you all say? Perhaps Elias has a point . . ."

Elias snapped with sudden agitation. "I don't need you to validate my thoughts. I care not for validation from you of any sort."

Moshe resumed his speech again, ignoring the interruption. "The Kommandant has given us until tomorrow morning. We must take advantage of it. And perhaps, God or someone else will enlighten us with an answer."

" 'The best fire doesn't flare up the soonest . . .' "

"Jiri, I don't see fires at the moment," Moshe said.

"Oh, but how *ignorant* you are . . . those are not my words, but the words of George Eliot, one of my favorite writers. And do you know why? Because in order to be read and appreciated, she was forced to sign her work using a man's name."

"Berkovitz?"

"I too am in favor of waiting it out. It's as if the commandant wanted to rush us. Do you all not get the feeling that he's toying with us? Perhaps we should do precisely what he wouldn't expect. And sooner or later, we'll need to find out exactly who he is," Berkovitz stated, pointing in the direction of the blond prisoner.

"Alexey?"

The Ukrainian obligingly turned toward Jacek, who in turn spoke for both of them.

"We agree to wait. I don't see the purpose in trying to rush a decision."

Otto rushed toward Moshe.

"Don't you understand! We—"

But a faint and debilitated whimper from the far end of the room forced Otto to stop.

"Moshe . . ."

The voice was tremulous. Feeble. It was Jan. Moshe and Berkovitz made their way to the dark corner and kneeled down next to the elderly man, who was lying on the floor. Jan gasped and his throat rattled with each word he spoke. His eyes were watering and his hands were emaciated. All of the inmates understood the signs.

"You mustn't keep arguing. There's no need," Jan spoke.

"But—"

With a wave of his hand the elderly man dismissed the petition.

"You must choose me."

Moshe resolutely shook his head.

"I would never let that happen, Jan. You—"

"I'm dying, Moshe. You know that. And so do you, Berkovitz."

"You all know . . . I've lost my will. I'm tired. I have no more energy. If I had the strength I would go myself before the SS officers. I want only for it to end."

"We'll find you some soup. That's all you need, Jan. Once you've eaten, you'll feel better."

The elderly man shook his head resolutely. "No, I don't want to eat. I don't want any of this anymore, Moshe. Leave me be. Allowing someone else to die would be a waste. At least, in this way, my death will have served some purpose. I will have saved all of you . . . and that is no small feat."

"Perhaps none of us will be executed. Perhaps—"

"Listen to me." But Jan was unable to finish; his body heaved with convulsions once again, violently afflicted by a fit of coughing. Death seemed to suddenly loom over him. The others looked on, silent. Slowly, his cough resided and his breathing seemed to regain a steady pace. From his lungs came a feeble hiss.

"I'm fifty-six years old. Out there, perhaps I'd still be of some use. I could still work, care for my family, plan for our future. But in here, it's hopeless. I feel as if I'm near a hundred. I won't make it."

Again, he coughed.

"We all know that only the youngest here have a chance to survive. Listen to me, Moshe, and tell the others. Call the commandant, tell him that you've chosen me. I believe the others will consent to it."

The effort to speak had weakened him completely. His eyes lost their luster, and Jan lay immobile across the blankets.

Moshe turned to Berkovitz.

"What now?" he whispered.

"It's terrible. But . . . he's right. Eight to one, it's a good exchange, considering."

Together, they returned to the table under the bleak flicker of the barren lightbulb.

"How is he?" Jacek asked.

"Not well. I don't think he has much time left. He says . . . he says that we should choose him."

Berkovitz gave no other explanation. Moshe knew what the others were feeling: boundless despair for having to make such a horrible choice, and at the same time, a euphoric sense of relief.

"But, of course!" Alexey was the only one who made known his satisfaction. "He wouldn't have made it anyway. He's a Muslim; he had no chance . . . one day more or less, what does it matter?"

He had voiced what all the others were thinking.

"All right then, come on. Let's call the guards and tell them!"

The others had not the courage to speak, nor to move. Only Otto continued with his pacing back and forth, back and forth in the dimly lit space near of the window.

"What are you doing?" Moshe erupted without warning, staring at Otto.

"What's that?"

"Otto, what are you doing? You've been pacing across the room for the last ten minutes. What are you doing?"

"Nothing. I'm just nervous. This calms me, somewhat."

"That may be true"—Moshe approached him—"or perhaps it isn't."

Moshe stood next to Otto, who followed him with his restless gaze.

"It might appear to be a trifling detail: a man pacing back and forth. What's odd about that?" Moshe glanced at each of the others. "Yet, if you were to look at the whole picture, what would you see? Imagine that the camp is completely dark, save only for the watchtowers. And the only window that casts light is our own. The other barracks have closed up for the night. And still, in this window, there is a silhouette of a figure walking back and forth. Not like this . . ."

Moshe took a few steps, crossing the room once and then back again in a normal stride.

"But rather, like this."

Moshe then replicated Otto's seemingly discordant pattern of movement: two paces forward, a pause, three more paces, pause, pace, pause.

"Now, if you add that particular detail into the whole equation, what do you see?"

He scanned the room, eyeing the silent onlookers.

"It's someone sending signals," Jacek stated coldly. The others turned in his direction.

"Precisely. Someone is sending signals. It wouldn't surprise me if it were in the form of Morse code, or something of that nature."

Otto had gone pale.

"You're mad. How could you ever suppose . . ."

Moshe drew nearer to Otto so that only a few inches of space separated the two. The Red was just as tall, yet of a sturdier and more robust build. Still, in that moment, Moshe felt that he was in control.

"There's nothing to suppose, Otto. One need only observe

and deduce. Tell us, Otto, who or what is out there, waiting for your signal?"

Otto tried to dismiss the accusation with a smile but only managed a grimace.

"You're all mad . . . why would I be sending signals to the outside? That's utter nonsense."

"Perhaps there is some SS out there busy relaying your messages to the commandant. This place is flush with spies, or have you not noticed? It could very well be that the entire escape was fabricated, and that the commandant has issued us here in order to find out something else entirely."

"You've all forgotten that I—"

"That you're a Red Triangle. We know. But, perhaps you struck a deal with the commandant. Perhaps Breitner is keen to know if there's any member of the *Kampfgruppe* hidden here within our barrack; who would be most inclined to come across such information? And a comrade nonetheless! I suppose at this point, that means very little. When your sort become part of the league of Kapos, they carry out their duties as fiercely as the others, if not more so. Beating after beating!"

Otto's face flushed with a livid red hue, but he did not reply.

Jiri made his way over to the two after having walked the perimeters of the room with his same sinuous gait.

"Do you know what the situation reminds me of? An old Jewish tale. Oh, you've most certainly heard it before," he said, directing his attention to Moshe, Berkovitz, and Elias. "But the others, perhaps not. Anyhow, the story goes that there once was a merchant from Budapest, and on the days that his business prospered, he would tell his wife to light a single candle. On the days that his business suffered, he would tell his wife to light every candle in every room of the house. One day, his wife, who had never understood this practice, asked him to explain. 'It's simple,'

he said. 'When my business suffers, so should the others. For when
they see our house aglow in the middle of the day, they'll imagine that I've acquired quite a sum of money. And yet, when things
are going well, I offer the others one simple little joy: they can take
pleasure in the belief that I must make do with but one solitary
candle.'"

Jiri recited the tale as if it were a monologue for the stage. His
closing words were followed by the same hush that descends on a
theater just as the curtain drops.

"Your little story is quite befitting," observed Moshe. "With
the exception of a few small details. First, there is no merchant
from Budapest here, but rather a Communist from—where are
you from, Otto?"

"From the Ruhr area."

"Yes, from the Ruhr area. Second, the man in the tale is mock-
ing his neighbors' needless envy, while here . . . Otto, to whom
were you sending those messages?"

The German glanced around the room. The others looked on
with an obvious distrust. Had they been forced to choose in that
moment, there was little doubt as to who would have been executed.

"All right," Otto said, heaving a sigh of submission after what
seemed an interminable silence. "I'll tell you everything."

He crossed to the window, then turned to face the others
with his back to the window and the darkness that lay beyond it.

"I am not a spy. I am the chief commander of the resistance."

He cast a piercing glance toward Jacek.

"Mark my words, if you tell the SS officers, you won't live to
see tomorrow. My comrades will slit your throat the instant that
the lights go out."

"You're not in a position to threaten anyone here, Otto,"
Moshe quipped. "Go on."

"We were the ones who organized the escape. We had discovered a way out, though the route I will not divulge. The escape three days ago was a trial run, and we succeeded. Now is the time for us to enact our plan. First, the party's key members must flee."

"Meaning you, I imagine," Jacek added.

"Yes, of course. Beginning with me. At the moment, we are in the midst of a large-scale operation."

"To steal a vat of *Wassersuppe?*" asked Moshe.

"We want at least ten comrades to escape this time. They are in the *Arbeitskommandos* and are working at Buna. They're willing to help the AK."

"And after that? You'll declare war on Luxembourg?"

"The war will be over in less than six months. It's vital that the party be rebuilt as quickly as possible. We are needed. Nothing of this sort should ever happen again in Germany."

"I see, so you're sacrificing yourself for the sake of Europe."

"It's an effort of many, not just one. We have been organizing for weeks now. They are waiting for me. It is for this reason that I've been trying to reach them. They need to know that I am still alive. The SS officers raided the camp just as the second escape was scheduled to get under way. Without me, the entire operation is at risk. By five o'clock tomorrow morning, I must be out of this place, one way or another."

Moshe listened with an air of skepticism, but remained silent. Berkovitz, too, seemed perplexed by all that had just occurred; he removed his glasses and took to rubbing the bridge of his nose once more. Jiri resumed his singing "*Sass ein Jäger mit seiner Lola.*" Meanwhile, Jacek and Alexey both eyed Otto with open hostility.

"You don't believe me," Otto declared.

"Convince us then," Moshe answered.

"Listen—in Germany, I was a medical student. My mother died when I was still very young. My father and my brother worked for Krupp Steel. It was backbreaking work, with ten- or even twelve-hour shifts every day. I was the smartest one in the family, and all their savings went toward putting me through university. I wanted to be a doctor. I wanted to be a phenomenal doctor. I would have treated the steelworkers' children for free; I would have accepted money only from those who could have afforded to pay something. Like all little children, I knew very little about the way in which the world worked."

Otto's complexion suddenly turned ashen.

"One day, there was an accident at the factory inside the smelting furnace. My brother was killed by the blast, and Father passed away five days later, having never regained consciousness. And then I was on my own. I had to give up my studies. I, too, went to work at the factory, but I have never forgotten either my brother or my father."

Silence descended again on the barrack.

"It's all very tragic," Moshe said. "But who is to say that any of it is true? To whom were you signaling? Why were we the nine chosen? Why were Aristarchos and the boy taken out? And who is he?" Moshe pointed to the blond man who had not spoken again.

"I'd say you're a spy," Moshe said, still targeting Otto.

"You—"

But he didn't have the chance to finish. Elias, who had fallen silent for some time, exploded with a sudden rage.

"A spy! You, of all people, you dare to accuse someone of such a thing . . . a *spy!*"

The Jewish man's face was contorted with fury. The others watched in bewilderment: Elias was known as a man of gentle nature, one who never raised his voice.

Moshe gave no reply. Instead, he stood with his eyes cast toward the floor in embarrassment. This, too, puzzled the others.

Normally, Moshe's confidence would have equipped him with banter to prevail in any situation.

"Traitor . . . cheater . . . snake!" howled Elias.

Jiri wrapped his arm around Elias's shoulder in an attempt to calm him, but was quickly shoved aside.

"It's time all of you knew about this man. He who has the nerve to accuse another of being a spy. He, of all people—how utterly ridiculous!"

No one dared speak. Even Jacek and Alexey seemed to have taken an interest. And even Otto, for a moment, had forgotten his own urgent matter.

"This man that you see here . . . Moshe Sirovich, a real estate agent by profession, known throughout the neighborhood and, I daresay, throughout all of Warsaw. I wouldn't say esteemed— if anything, feared. No one could do business quite like him. A wolf in sheep's skin, I daresay—"

"Elias—" Moshe pleaded, glancing up for a brief instant.

"Shut up, you mongrel. You're nothing but a traitor who was mistaken for a saint, just like Jesus. You have the ability to sway anyone with your words. Or am I lying? No, I'm most certainly not. How often did you swindle those in your business dealings? Gentiles or Jews: for you it mattered little. And yet we admired you for it. Even I admit to having been fascinated by your deftness, your skills. Fascinated to the point that I . . . trusted you. I trusted you! The greatest mistake I ever made!"

"They aren't interested in that, Elias."

"Perhaps not before, no. But now . . . now they need to know who and what is here. You accused Otto of being a spy. I don't know if that's true. But I do know that you would betray even your dearest friend. And that is something they do need to know. Now it *is* important."

Elias wiped his mouth with the back of his hand. Thirst was starting to show its teeth. The only means of hydration within the camp was the soup. But as of yet, no one had brought them anything to eat.

"Back in Warsaw, by the time they had detained us in the ghetto, Moshe had become a friend of mine. In truth, I would say my dearest friend. A few months before that, I had profited from a very good deal he made; I attributed this to what I then deemed his good nature. I had become so blind that I could not grasp that it was all a plan, and nothing more."

"*Timeo Danaos et dona ferentes,*" Jiri recited.

"Don't interrupt," barked Alexey. "No one wants to hear your Romanian proverbs."

"My dearest friend, I told you. Often, my wife and I would invite him to our home. Two or three times a week he would have dinner with us. My family and I welcomed him, offering him every comfort and privilege as if he were an important visitor. I was ever so clouded by his pleasantries and his confidence, that I confess there was a time . . . yes, there was a time when I dreamed of becoming just like him. I studied his gestures, his speech, his movement, even his smile. We were all so taken by him. Even my daughter, until the . . ." For a moment his words were lost, drowned out by a sudden surge of despair. "And my wife. Yes, she more than anyone."

For a moment, Elias ceased to speak. The room was silent.

"You must all already know how this tale will end. Just like that. Don't you see? His shameless nature knows no bounds. Right there in front of me. I was a laughingstock in the ghetto . . . and I was the last to know."

Jiri's eyes flashed maliciously, yet he dared not speak a word. Nor did the others. Only Alexey erupted in a wicked fit of laughter.

"Wouldn't you know it? Our Moshe, the shrewd and crafty dealer, is quite a resourceful man."

"Who spends his days cutting deals with the Nazis, you mustn't forget that," Jacek added.

"Shut up," Moshe said. "You are definitely not one to speak on the matter."

Elias seemed to have regained his composure; now that he had shaken what had weighed so heavily upon his heart, he felt calm and at ease once again.

"I told you because I wanted you all to know who this man is and what he is capable of. I would be wary of trusting him."

"And it isn't you that I blame," Moshe said as he turned to the man who had once been his dear friend.

"Did I lie?" the rabbi asked.

"No, you didn't lie. But you also haven't told the whole truth. You've asked the others to judge me on the very night that we must choose one of our own to die. It is important that they know all sides to this story. All sides, without question."

"There's nothing you could tell that could alter the judgment that will befall you."

"That might be true. But, I shall have to try. It's true, Elias, I betrayed your trust. I am at fault, and perhaps you will find relief in knowing that I will never forgive myself. But you have forgotten that during that period, your wife suffered from a most acute form of depression, and that you were the cause."

Elias placed the palms of his hands squarely over his ears. His eyes were squeezed tightly closed.

"Shut up! Enough! Make him stop! I will not listen to these lies!"

Moshe crossed to where Elias now stood. He then took both of Elias's hands by the wrist and forced them to release their grip.

"No. You must listen. This way, you can attest to whether or not it is the whole truth."

Moshe turned toward the others. Elias remained behind him; grief-stricken, he let his arms drop limply to his sides.

"They welcomed me into their home; it's true. And I went, as a friend would do. And it's also true that not long after, I made advances on his wife, Myriam. But I never would have dared touch her had . . . had it not been for the tragic events that came to pass. Myriam and Elias had a daughter, Ida. She was eight years old. She was lovely and sweet, with blond hair much like her mother's. She used to call me 'Uncle.' And when I would walk through their door, she would shout, 'Uncle Moshe!' and throw her arms around my neck. I always brought her sweets, or some little gift. Even in the ghetto I never had problems procuring a little something here or there."

"What did I tell you?" Elias interrupted. "He used the most sneaky means of finding a place in our home and winning our affections."

Moshe took no notice of the outburst.

"We knew we were in danger. There were many that clung to the delusion that the ghetto would be their permanent residence. Others saw their fate all too clearly. Our community, confined to that small area, become ever more united. It was a comfort to see our only friends and acquaintances on the street each day, while elsewhere . . . elsewhere there were Nazis setting the world ablaze. Many had come to believe that perhaps they'd leave us alone, confined to our neighborhood until the war was over."

"And that is the very reason for which we find ourselves here. Our optimism allowed us to miscalculate," observed Berkovitz.

"We had not yet understood the dangers, until it was altogether too late. But I had sources, and I knew what the Nazis had in mind. And so, I warned Elias and Myriam. I begged them to save themselves. There was still time. But Elias was, as usual, relentlessly stubborn. He preferred to leave their fate in the hands of God. At the time, I too could have escaped. But I could not bear to be apart from Myriam. For the first time in my life, I chose to reject reason and listen only to my heart."

"You have no heart," snarled Elias.

"Even though I knew he would oppose, I had found a way for Ida to escape. A pretty little blond girl would not have had difficulty passing as Aryan. There was a Catholic family willing and waiting to welcome her into their home. She was to join the family as their niece having just arrived from Silesia. Perhaps they could even have found her the right treatment."

Elias's eyes suddenly brightened.

"What treatment?" Berkovitz queried.

"She had something in her bone marrow, something that had to do with her white blood cells. The doctors said there was no hope for her, right, Elias?"

The rabbi didn't reply but simply shrugged. His grief had overwhelmed him.

"But we had heard that in Berlin or maybe in America, they had made a breakthrough, using something called X-rays. And perhaps when the war was finally over, we could have taken her there."

"Ida was not meant to live," Elias spoke in a voice barely above a whisper. "God wanted it that way."

"But it wasn't that severe. Not then anyway. She was a little pale, but no one would have suspected an illness of any sort. I had, at any rate, managed to procure the necessary documents. With the help of a few gold watches and a couple of diamonds, I was able to strike a deal with one of the guards. Ida was to leave the ghetto hidden away in the hearse of a funeral procession; after which she would be taken to her new family. Myriam had consented to the plan, and even though the thought of death lay heavy on her heart—it was not easy for her to be separated, for who knows how long, from her own daughter—still, she had agreed to it. The night of Ida's escape arrived. And at the very last minute, he"—Moshe pointed toward Elias—"broke it off. He said something about God, and Abraham, and I don't know what else, and refused to let her go. We begged and pleaded, Myriam and I. And it amounted to nothing. He was unwavering. He couldn't bear the idea that his daughter would have to pass as a Catholic. He said that God would never forgive him, and that he could never betray his God . . . the same God who brought you here, right, Elias? At daybreak, the guard was relieved of his post, and after that, there was nothing we could do. Fifteen days later, they came to the ghetto. They carried us off. Upon leaving the train, one of the officers on the ramp separated Ida from both Myriam and Elias. And after that, she was gone."

Elias doubled over, wheezing, and if he could have, had the KZ not dried up his tears, he would have cried.

"That's what really happened. That's how Elias's family was reduced to this. Ida disappeared and Myriam . . . after that, she began to hate him. She couldn't stand the thought of his touch. After a while, he ceased to exist. But beneath her hatred, Myriam suffered. She suffered more than she could bear."

"And you thought that you ought to be the one to comfort her, right?" Elias had pulled himself together and was filled with rage. "Look!" From beneath his crude and tattered jacket, he pulled out a crumpled photograph and showed it to the others.

"Ida. My little Ida."

The prisoners looked at the photo. Ida was small and thin, with long blond plaits in her hair and a smile that seemed to show infinite sadness.

"You're mad," Berkovitz declared, "Keeping a photograph hidden like that. They'll beat you if they find it. That's quite a futile risk you're taking."

Elias only shrugged. He held the photograph delicately in his hand. He raised it to his lips, kissed it gently, and placed it once again inside his jacket.

"She is the only person in the world who never betrayed me."

"Enough," Otto snapped. "Enough of this trivial bourgeois melodrama. We're in a KZ. There's no use in wallowing in our past regrets. We're beyond that now. We must think only of the present."

Jacek took a step forward. "Good, very good. Let's see here: we have a Red Triangle suspected of espionage; a Jew renowned for trafficking who betrayed his own best friend; another Jew, though a devout one, who thwarted every effort to save his own daughter and then threw his own wife into the arms of his colleague; a homosexual who sells himself to the *Prominenten* in exchange for favors; a rich Jewish financier who, until the very end, did business with the Nazis; an elderly Jew on the verge of death—"

"You forgot the Polish criminal who spies for the commandant along with his aide who took his fist to each and every face you see here," Moshe added. "Yes, you're right: the difficulty in choosing a victim lies in the abundance of good choices."

"You're mistaken," Berkovitz interjected. "You noted eight people, but there are nine of us here. You missed him." He pointed to the blond man.

"You're right," Jacek assented. "I think it's time we find out who he is. Perhaps we'll find that we're in good company."

They approached the blond man who had remained silent since his arrival. Yet, before they were able to ask him a single question, the door to the barrack swung open once more.

2000 Hours

The Oberscharführer stood in the door frame with his legs far apart.

"The commander wants to know if you've chosen."

"You gave us until tomorrow morning," Berkovitz said. "And what would be the time now?"

"Twenty hundred hours."

"And our soup? We have not eaten since this morning."

"You may place an official complaint. You will need a WH11 form. You must send it to the *Blockältester* in charge who will deliver it to the *Lagerältester*." The Oberscharführer laughed at his own joke. "They will bring you soup at some point. At this moment, there are other matters to which we must attend."

The warrant officer then turned toward the exit. He signaled to the guards posted outside.

The nine *Häftlinge* held their breath.

At first, the light brought the glimpse of only a hand into view. Thin, frail, almost translucent fingers. Then an arm, which seemed to swim in the wide expanse of the striped sleeve.

A woman. She looked around with uncertainty, her vision

obscured by the bleak light from the barren bulb. Both Moshe and Elias grew pale.

"Myriam," Moshe called out. Elias, overwhelmed by the sight, spoke not a word. He stood in silence, his jaw trembling.

The woman remained mute and stock-still in the center of the room. Her uniform enveloped her, hanging about her body, her emaciated limbs just barely visible. Her hair had been cut very short and lay in uneven tufts about her head. The electric razor, as usual, had proved to do a very shoddy job. Her eyes bulged from two cavernous sockets, her cheeks wan and haggard. Only a faint flutter of her eyelids revealed her anguished state.

"Good, very good," the Oberscharführer remarked. "I see you're already acquainted. Then you're in good company. Camp regulations prohibit the joint confinement of men and women, but we will make an exception this time. If you have complaints, you may file form KK206."

He exited without another word, closing the door behind him. The *Häftlinge* found themselves alone. Again, there were ten.

"Myriam," Moshe repeated and took a step toward her. An instant later, Elias moved as well, but when he realized Moshe had already stepped forward, he turned on his heel and walked to the opposite side of the room.

"Myriam," Moshe said again when he found himself facing her.

Alexey smirked with contentment.

"Ah, the local tart has arrived," he sneered.

At that very moment, the blond man, who had remained utterly mute, suddenly sprang to his feet with a wild expression on his face.

"Ruhe, Schwein!"

Alexey found himself cornered by Paul, who stood menacingly jabbing his finger into Alexey's chest, articulating the words:

Я ПРЕДСТАВАЛЁЮ СЕБЕ НА ПОСАЛІ В
ПЕРМАН – СЬКОМУ ПРАВЛіННі. ЯКІЦО
ДОТРОНИШСЯ ДО ЦіЕі ЖіНКИ ЦЕ РАЗ, ТО
ЗРОБЛαSЮ З ТЕБЕ КіНЕЦЬ В КАМіНі. ЗРО-
ЗУМі В?

Alexey's skin had turned a pallid hue. He stood mute, his eyes cast downward, his usual arrogance suddenly stripped away. Confused, the others watched his sudden shift in behavior.

"What did he say to you?" Jacek asked.

Alexey only shook his head.

Meanwhile, Moshe reached out his hand to touch Myriam's face, but just as he neared her, she pushed it sharply away.

"Leave me alone!"

"Myriam, you don't understand. We—"

"I know everything. The Herr Oberscharführer explained everything. You must choose someone by tomorrow morning."

"We had just been talking about it. We—"

"Do what you want," she interceded. "It doesn't matter. Nothing matters anymore, don't you see?" She drew away, crossing the room, thrusting aside the uniforms drying on the line, and slipping into one of the dark corners of the barrack. Moshe started to follow her.

"No," said Elias. "Let her be. You have already caused her too much pain."

Giving no regard to his instructions, Moshe continued his pursuit, but Elias seized him by the wrist, his eyes burning with a frenzied rage.

"No!"

Moshe shook his head and retreated toward the others.

During that time, Jacek had covered the windows using some of the sheets in the barrack.

"At least this way we will know that it is for only those of us here to decide."

Otto protested, "You could be jeopardizing the entire escape! You mustn't! You—"

"Jacek is right," Berkovitz intervened. "Until we are certain that no one here is a spy, it is better to act prudently."

Otto started in, as if to dispatch his protests once again, but then abandoned his efforts.

"Now then," Jacek inquired, "what are going to do?"

"You see, Felix, a vast majority of people would argue that chess is a metaphor for the perfect battle."

The little boy arranged his pieces on the board without much interest in his father's complicated explanations.

"It's true, of course; an ideal battle would consist of two opposing forces, equal in every aspect, the only advantage being that the whites are permitted to advance first."

The commander pointed to the knight.

"Everything depends upon the skill and strength of the commander." He heaved a sigh. "However, in the real world, that is not always the case. Do you know what Napoleon used to say? That he preferred a lucky general to a good one. You see, luck is often considered a fundamental element. And while it certainly requires tenacity and hard work to reach the finish line, it takes but a little thing to destroy it all."

Breitner stared into space. He thought again of the news that had come from the front lines.

"But chess does not refer only to the battlefield," he resumed. "It also represents men. Take the knight, for example." He picked up the piece and held it out for the boy to see. "The knight is the only piece that can move in two different directions at the same time. The knight is the one piece that circles you, hinders your balance, and strikes when you are least prepared. He is the soldier with uncalculated resources, who will seize you unaware, who never travels a straight route but prefers the more tortuous paths."

Breitner placed the piece back on the board. He picked up another.

"The rook is a different case altogether, for he is a fearless warrior, one of strength and courage. But, ah, he is predictable. His path is a linear one; he journeys ahead never stopping for anyone. His flaw lies in his inability to adapt, to change strategies. In short, he lacks imagination."

Felix had now taken an interest. The little boy grabbed hold of one of the pieces.

"And what about the bishop, Papa? The bishop goes straight too."

Breitner smiled.

"Oh no, Felix. It's true, the movement of the bishop appears to be much like that of the rook. Yet, the bishop never moves in straight line, no, rather his path is crooked and oblique. While the bishop cannot travel right or left in the same manner as the knight, his movements are of the most treacherous. The moment you turn your back, you will feel his wrath. It is but for his duplicitous movements that he is able to penetrate the most impervious of defenses . . . and that is something the rook cannot do."

Felix weighed the black bishop in his hand, eyeing it with skepticism. He did not like the bishop.

"And the pawns, Papa?"

"The pawns are just meat on the butcher's block. Simple soldiers. But you must still be wary, for they are the only pieces that do not capture in the same way that they move. They move in a forward motion, but destroy in a diagonal path. Much like if foot soldiers were equipped with machine guns: it could become rather perilous."

Breitner picked up another piece.

"And then there's the queen."

"Yes, she is very powerful, Papa. More powerful than the others."

"You're right. She is the most precious. It is for this very reason that you must keep her safe; you mustn't lose her. You must not subject her to open combat. The queen will only attack when she is ready. Or when there is no other alternative."

The little boy gazed reverently at the last piece.

"You forgot the king, Papa."

"Yes, of course, the king."

Breitner held the piece up to his face, as if seeing it for the first time.

"The king. The unequivocal object of the game."

"But he can't do anything, Papa. Isn't that strange?"

"You're right, Felix. He moves only one square at a time. He is so very weak and powerless that castling was created, a special move that protects the king and his defenses."

"But shouldn't the king be the most powerful of all?"

"He is, Felix. But the king is not simply the piece that commands the soldiers on the battlefield. He is much more than that. The king represents the ideals for which we fight. He is the Holy Grail, the final acquisition, the end to the means of every war. He is neither a person, nor simply a piece, but rather something we hold to be exceptionally important. It is this very reason for which we are now at war."

Breitner turned toward the window and peered into the darkness that hung about the camp, as if searching to validate his words. He could see only the reflections cast from the watchtowers. He returned his focus to the board, setting the king back in position.

"Very well, then," he sighed. "I think we can begin."

"All right then, what do you think?" the former barrack leader continued.

"Do what you want. It bears little consequence for me," Otto said flatly.

"How so?"

Otto ignored him. Instead, he turned to address the others.

"I am far too crucial a factor in our plan. I have no choice; I must live. Not for my own sake, but for the sake of the future, our future."

His words were met with silence. After a few seconds, Berkovitz spoke.

"We'll sort all of that out later, given there are any number of doubts regarding your story. Still, if we're keeping score, I'd say, Why not Alexey? We all know who we're dealing with, given that every one of us has taken a beating from him."

"Don't even try it," Alexey said. He pulled his knife from his jacket once again. "Whoever moves first gets their throat cut. What goes for me, goes for him too," he snarled through clenched teeth, pointing in the direction of Jacek. This time, Jacek did nothing to stop him.

Elias suddenly spoke.

"As for me, I have no doubts." His voice trembled. "I told you our story, mine and Myriam's. Perhaps it is of no consequence to you here in the camp. So, then let's talk of the camp; you know it well. And you know just as well that Moshe traffics with the Nazis every day. He doesn't hate them, he does business with them. And who is to know if we are involved in these dealings. I don't

know how it is that he manages to procure all those goods from
the Kanada: watches, jewelry, grappa, cigars. He could buy all
the bread and soup he wanted, and even margarine if he pleased!
I'd hardly be surprised to learn that the SS officers let him visit
cell twenty-nine from time to time. You like the Polish girls, eh,
Moshe. A man of his kind knows no limits. You all must know
this. I do not trust him."

Moshe shook his head. "It's true; I do business with the jackboots," he conceded, looking each of the prisoners in the eye. "In
Warsaw, I was a real estate agent. It was in my nature to barter and
trade with people; I'd cut deals with anyone. In my line of work,
you have to know how to read people: who they are, what they
want, what they like, what they don't. Often, they don't even
know what they're after, so you have to be the one to tell them.
But the trick is to make them believe that they came to that decision on their own. And in that way, you get just what you're after.
It's not any different in here."

As he spoke he slowly circled the table. "The jackboots are
experts at warfare, but not business. Business affairs are done for
them, by people like myself or like him." He pointed to Berkovitz. "And so, every day, I do my job. Because I want precisely
the same thing as all of you—to survive."

He stood still, having found himself in the same spot in which
he had started. "And what is the harm in that? Should I have
evaded all contact with the enemy? Should I have preferred death
so that I might have maintained my—what are you calling it?—
my dignity?"

No one answered.

"Do you truly think that if I refused their business—the bread,
the soup, and even the cigarettes—that the Russians would have
already come to liberate us? Do you think that my deals prevented
the fall of Berlin? Or rather, that I would not be dead already?

I would be at the *kremchy*, waiting to be thrown alive into the crematorium. And so yes, perhaps the jackboots have a few extra gold watches—"

Elias, having listened indignantly to Moshe's speech, interrupted him.

"He steals from the dead, you mustn't forget that! From those who have been burned alive. From the women who arrive at the ramp without knowing a thing!"

"Yes, from them too," Moshe admitted. "Were you ever even there at the ramp? No. All right then, I'll tell you what happens. The *Häftlinge*, like those of us here, comfort them, give them support, and tell them that everything is going to be just fine. The women and children go here, the men over there. 'Don't worry my friends, in a short while you'll be reunited with your family again. After the shower . . .'"

"You . . . you . . ." Elias struggled in vain to find the right word.

"Am I a monster? Perhaps. I did it, just as many others have. You too, Berkovitz, am I right? You were there at the ramp. And you told them that everything would be all right. Isn't that so, Berkovitz?"

The prisoner gave no answer.

Moshe turned once again to Elias.

"And do you know why we said the things we did? Because warning them would be a futile effort. They would have burned either way, and we—"

"You would have been beaten."

"Or killed. With a shot to the neck. And so now, tell me, Rabbi: Did I err in my ways? What, I pray, does the Talmud preach regarding the matter? Or had they forgotten to compile that chapter?"

From one of the far corners of the room, Jiri unleashed a slow applause.

"Bravo. Well done. When the *Kabarett* reopens, I'll hire you as a writer."

The Pink Triangle gave a quick turn before moving across the room, making his way past the curtains. Through the slight aperture between the fabrics, Moshe watched as Jiri approached Myriam. He took a seat next to her, atop a blanket. He gently, and with great reserve, stroked her short tufts of hair, to which she made no protest.

"You poor thing," Jiri said, "how you must have suffered."

Alexey had followed the scene with a contentious smile on his face. He then turned, and looked at the others at the table. Paul was a good distance away. He appeared distracted.

"And if we choose her?" he whispered so as not to attract the attention of the blond man.

"You're mad!" Moshe exploded.

"Come on . . . we all know that a woman's chances of surviving are slim here. Look at her. Not to mention, she's a Muslim. She won't last but a few weeks. So—"

"Shut up, Alexey. I won't have you dragging Myriam into this. Elias, tell him . . ."

Elias stood, mute. He bit his lips, offering no reply.

"There's no use in being sentimental," Alexey carried on contemptuously. "The weakest one should go. And she's the weakest."

"Shut up!" Moshe warned, "If you keep this up—"

He stopped short. From behind them, Myriam appeared. Silence saturated the room. The woman approached them. She placed her palms on the table. The bleak light seemed to deepen her eye sockets even more. Jiri followed a short distance behind.

"You were talking about me."

"We . . ." Elias began, embarrassed.

"There's no need. I already know."

"No!" Elias's face flushed red. "It was Alexey. He . . . he isn't human."

"And why is that?" Myriam asked. "He's right. I am the weakest one here. It's only fair that I be sent to the wall."

"There, see," Alexey said. "She said it herself. Good then! I think we're all in agreement here, so there's nothing left to discuss." As he spoke he stroked the handle of his knife.

"Scheiße!"

From his corner in the room, the blond bounded forth like a loaded spring. He first disarmed Alexey with a swift and fierce kick, and then threw himself at him.

"Schwein!" Paul roared as he grabbed Alexey's neck in a choke hold. "You want to condemn a woman! Coward!"

The sudden attack left the colossal Ukrainian in a state of shock, though the worst was yet to come. He writhed and twisted on the floor, struggling to free himself of the grip that now impeded his every effort to breathe. His face took on a blue hue; his body fell limp. The others watched, frozen by the violent brawl that transpired in the silent space, except for the suffocated snarls of the two adversaries. Myriam was the only one to approach them.

"Enough!" she ordered. "Enough!"

And when the two failed to cease their fighting, she sent forth a kick, striking the tangled mess of limbs.

"Enough!"

Paul, realizing that the woman now stood over them, released his grip. Alexey slinked away; he recovered his knife and secured it once again in the fold of his jacket. His lungs wheezed as they struggled for air. With one hand, he rubbed his neck, reddened from the attack. Paul rose to his feet. In the brawl, his jacket sleeve had been pushed back just above his elbow so that his forearm was exposed. Moshe stared at Paul's naked arm, dumbstruck.

"You . . ."

He took a step closer to Paul. Before he could react, Moshe grabbed him by the wrist, showing the others his exposed arm.

"Look!"

An *A+* had been etched into his arm.

Berkovitz and the others went pale with fright. Jiri, without realizing it, moved back.

Paul pulled his sleeve back down to his wrist, covering his arm.

"That's right. Paul Hauser, Hauptsturmführer of the SS," he clicked his heels once in salute.

Moshe, too, had turned ashen.

"Why are you here?"

The blond man smiled. The fact that the others had discovered his true identity did not seem to trouble him.

"I fought on the eastern front. In Ukraine."

"Ladies!" howled Jiri. "We have ourselves a real war hero!"

Paul ignored the jab.

"But then," Moshe asked, "how is it that you ended up here with us?"

"Insubordination."

Berkovitz weighed the officer's remark.

"What happened?"

"We were stationed in Ukraine, where according to the Reichsführer's orders, we were to seize and lay claim to the space that would occupy *Großdeutschland*. The influx of German immigrants had been well received, but as for the Jews . . . you already know. Initially, it was a bit of a blunder, we were ill prepared. The continuous shootings, the search and seizures, all of it was done at random. There was far too much bloodshed, too many screams, too many escapes . . . too much confusion. Dante's hell would have been more pleasant. One day, my platoon was ordered to execute a thousand Jews from a little village. We forced them to climb down into the holes that they themselves had dug, and they were shot, exterminated right there. We carried on like that for hours, in an indescribable state of confusion. Shots fired at random, the wounded writhing and crying out for help, the children crying as they clung to their mothers who lay dying beside them. My soldiers were forced to drink themselves into a stupor in order to carry on."

Paul's voice began to crack.

"I came undone. I abandoned my men and I left. The Standartenführer ordered me to return to my post, but I refused. 'The Jews are an inferior race,' I told him, 'it has been proven in both scientific and historical research. It is precisely for this reason that they will eventually die out on their own. They are weak, defenseless . . . things will take their due course. There is no need to slaughter them in this manner. It is beneath us. The German army fights to ensure that good is diffused throughout the land, as is the hope and will of the German people. . . . What will the world think of us?' "

"The Standartenführer would have been pleased."

"He let me speak and then he reminded me of the Reichsführer's orders. He, too, admitted that he was weary of the grievous methods we had been forced to implement, but we had no choice. The Russians wanted to prevent the expansion of *Großdeutschland,* and the Jews had control of the Soviet Union. And without sabotaging the efforts of the Jews, there was no other means. Those were the orders: exterminate them. And so I asked to be relieved of my post. I borrowed a service car and tried to make my way back to Berlin. I had hoped to speak with Himmler, to convince him to halt the operation. A hundred miles later, I was stopped. Desertion. They wanted to execute me then and there, but thanks to my connections, I was spared. My father is a major general, he did what he could."

Berkovitz rubbed his forehead, perplexed. "Your story might explain how it is that you were sent here, but it doesn't explain how you ended up in this barrack with all of us who have been sentenced to die."

Paul fixed his jacket, heaving an indignant sigh. "I had trouble here, too. I never got used to it. I didn't like the way the commander ran the camp. Stealing and being forced to steal. For himself and his men. You all know much better than I. It isn't befitting of a German officer. It's contemptible. He steals goods that are meant for the German people. With the help of a few friends, I managed to send word of his dealings to Berlin. Breitner found out and has not forgiven me. He couldn't extradite me, given my father's rank, so he decided to wait until an appropriate opportunity arose."

"Well, I'd say given the situation, our dilemma has been resolved," Otto declared. "We have here an SS officer among us. There's no need for further discussion. Call the Oberscharführer."

"In a bit of a rush to leave here, aren't you?" Paul asked wryly. "You would even have let a woman face execution just to leave this barrack. Spineless, cowardly Communists."

"All right, slow down," Moshe interjected. "It was Alexey's idea to choose Myriam. I assure you that no one here would have allowed it. We're not animals. You may indulge yourself with that thought and try as you may, but you have not yet reduced us to that state."

"Good then, we've agreed?" Otto carried on. "We'll name Paul; he seems the obvious choice." Without another word, he headed in the direction of the door.

"Go ahead. Call the commander and tell him that you've decided to have me executed." Hauser smiled.

"Precisely," Otto replied as he reached for the door.

"Wait a minute," Berkovitz said. "Just wait a minute."

"What is it?" Otto said, agitated by the interruption.

"Let's just think about this a moment," said the ex-financier. "We need to weigh out each of the particulars. Take a look at him." He pointed at Paul.

"What do you mean?"

"Take a good look. He's wearing a jacket, made of soft, thick leather. Have any of you ever come across something like this inside the camp? Moshe, you would know. Have you seen one like this?"

Moshe shook his head. "Even I don't think I could manage to score something of the sort, and if I did, I certainly couldn't go around wearing it. The SS would annihilate me."

"Exactly. What else? I'd say that Paul is rather well fed. Just look at how strong he still appears to be. Even his skin looks healthy. He's even wearing boots."

Even with only the bleak light cast from the bulb, it was clear that the former SS officer had enjoyed certain privileges within the camp.

"Well done," Paul commended, "you're beginning to get the picture."

"What's your point, Berkovitz? We're just wasting time here."

Moshe crossed the room to the exit and placed his palm securely over the door, blocking the politician's efforts to open it.

"Berkovitz is right, Otto. How is it that Paul walks around in that jacket eating his share of margarine every day?"

"I don't know. I-I . . ." Otto stammered, perplexed.

Paul wore a defiant grin. "Go on. Call the commander. I'm waiting."

"I don't think it's a good idea. It's obvious that Paul is well protected within the camp."

"Well done, Jew. You've managed to sort it out. It's quite true: your race is a weak but rather astute one. Do you really think that Breitner would have me shot; an Aryan SS officer, son of a major general whose close friend and confidant is none other than Wilhelm Keitel, and would in turn, spare you Jews? What justification could they give if and when word reached Berlin? Breitner's already under investigation for theft, he wouldn't risk being exposed of another blunder."

"But he did send you here to the barrack, thrown in with all of us."

Paul huffed dismissively. "He means to scare me, and probably aims to strike some sort of deal with me. Either way, he won't go through with this; it's much too dangerous, even for him."

Deep in thought, Otto moved away from the door and returned to the center of the room. Paul continued his discourse.

"And if you were to go out and call the Oberscharführer, what do you think would happen? The commander would have me executed and exonerate the nine of you, or better yet. . . ."

The room was silent. Each of the prisoners quietly weighed the risks against every possible outcome. At camp, nothing was ever as it seemed. The SS officers relished in deluding the prisoners. During certain selections, the officers would call out the numbers of those prisoners destined for the crematorium; at other times they would call out those whose lives were to be spared. The *Häftlinge* were never sure of their intentions. And this constant uncertainty heightened their fragility.

"All right already!" Otto erupted. "Either way, we must come to a decision. We're wasting time."

"Let it be wasted then," Moshe resounded. "No one cares about your escape. You and your party have nothing for us here.

You think only of the arrival of the Russians and of what will befall us after the war has ended. Meanwhile, the crematoriums still billow with smoke."

"It's nearing nine," Berkovitz stated. "We still have a few hours. Let's wait."

From the darkness came a noise. Myriam rushed to where Jan lay, struggling to breathe. She shifted his arms and legs, hoping to relieve his discomfort. She ran her palm over his brow. She then crossed to the utility sinks, where she dampened one corner of her uniform with the little water that dripped from the faucet. She returned to the elderly man and placed the damp cloth on his forehead. Jan smiled with gratitude.

"Thank you."

The prisoners had each followed the scene in silence. Jacek spoke first.

"And now we're back where we started."

The others, embarrassed, shifted their glances.

"I don't know that we have any other choice," he continued.

Otto heaved a sigh. "Jacek is right. It's terrible, but . . . it's the only way."

"Because elevated political thought would dictate that we should condemn the defenseless elderly, right?" asked Moshe.

"That isn't so. But it remains our sole solution," Berkovitz argued. "Jan is not well. He won't last much longer. And even if he manages to survive his illness, his future is settled. He is too old. It is the only logical choice."

"You mean to say," Jiri began, "that we should condemn an innocent elderly man in order to save an SS officer who massacred thousands of women and children? Forgive me, could you explain it again? I'm afraid I didn't quite follow."

Jan began to cough again, a convulsive, frenetic, and savage cough. The sound saturated the barrack.

"What did I tell you? He hasn't got much time left," Alexey said flatly.

"Alexey is right. We have no choice but to choose Jan."

Berkovitz sighed. "It's all we can do."

"Otto?" Jacek asked.

The politician cast his eyes away from the others. Then he nodded.

"Elias?"

"I will never give you a name. I will choose neither Jan nor Paul."

"Jiri?"

"Don't ask me . . . I beg you, don't ask me. . . ."

"Jiri?"

"I want no part. Don't you understand? I won't!" His voice was piercing.

"Jiri?"

"All right then, you vile brute, then yes, my vote is for Jan! There, I said it."

"Moshe?"

"Jan."

"Paul?"

The German shrugged.

Jacek turned to face the dark corner of the room.

"Someone call Myriam. She must vote too."

As he spoke, Myriam drew aside the uniforms that divided the room and made her way to where the men now stood. On her face was a look of devastation.

"Jan is dead," she said.

"Hello? Yes, you were saying, Herr Oberscharführer? The old man, yes, I see. Leave him there. *Heil Hitler!*"

Breitner placed the receiver back atop the telephone. He appeared lost in thought.

"Papa . . ."

"Yes, Felix?"

"The game . . . it's your turn."

"The game, yes."

The commander returned a momentary focus to the game; rather than resuming his seat, he stood as he studied the board.

"There."

With a quick flick of the wrist, he substituted one piece for another. The bishop took the place of the black pawn, which was returned to the chess box.

"You ate my pawn!" squealed Felix.

"Yes, I did. But I had no choice."

"Wait a minute, Papa, but couldn't the pawn escape?"

"The pawns are weak, Felix. They move from one square to the next, when they find that they are barricaded or that their path has been blocked, they give up moving altogether. They are not difficult to take down, for they are quite an easy mark."

The little boy winced. "I don't want to be a pawn."

Breitner sighed. "No, it isn't nice to be a pawn. In life, there is always that chance. But bear in mind one thing, Felix: even a most miserable and dejected pawn can transform itself into a queen."

"How?"

"You just have to get to the other side of the board. If you can manage to reach even the periphery of the enemy's camp, you can become whatever you wish."

The little boy studied the squadron of pieces that stood between the square once occupied by the pawn and the other half of the board.

"He never could have made it."

"No, not him. In any case, it's too late. But there are many pawns in this game. One of them could always evade the watchful eyes of the others, slip away unnoticed, hidden in the dark, and infiltrate the enemy's lines without anyone ever realizing. The rooks, the bishops, the knights, the queens . . . these are the pieces to which we usually pay the most attention. Pawns are just simple soldiers of little importance. But even a simple soldier can bring triumph to the battlefield."

Felix still studied the board, seemingly more perplexed than convinced.

"They are so sad, Papa. All just the same."

The commander smiled. "But the pieces *must* be all the same. They are soldiers, and soldiers are all the same. For this reason, they wear their uniform."

"Let's give them names then!"

"But the pieces—" Breitner stopped himself midsentence. "All right then. On one condition: I choose their names."

"What do you want to call them?"

"Let's start with the one that was just captured."

He took the pawn and held it up. The base of the piece was covered by a pale-colored cloth. From his desk, he took a fountain pen and wrote the name: *Jan.*

"Why Jan, Papa?"

"It's a name just like any other. But it seems to fit, wouldn't you say?"

Felix agreed.

"And this knight here, we'll call him Moshe."

"That's nice! It's a little strange, but I like it. Like Moses who crossed the Red Sea? I always liked that story from the Bible."

"Precisely."

The commander wrote *Moshe* on the cloth at the base of the knight.

One after the other, Breitner baptized the pieces while Felix assisted, approving or critiquing the names given. One pawn, Elias. Another pawn, Alexey. Then a bishop, Jiri. A rook, Otto. Another rook, Paul. A knight, Berkovitz. A bishop, Jacek.

Breitner then picked up the queen.

"Can we call her Frieda, Papa? Like Mom!"

His father grinned.

"Oh no, Felix! Even the queen could be eaten, and we wouldn't want anyone eating Mom, would we?"

"You're right! And Mom would not be good to eat. I like chicken better anyway!"

"Good then, we'll call the queen Myriam. Yes, that sounds like a name fit for a queen, doesn't it?"

"Who was Myriam, Papa?"

"According to the Bible, she was the sister of Moses."

"I want a sister too, Papa!"

"Felix, do you still want to play or are you too tired?"

The little boy gave a shrug. "If I go down now, Mommy will make me set the table."

Breitner unleashed a chuckle. "You know, in the barracks they call that shirking. Come on, let's go down together, I'll give you a hand. I believe that dinner is ready."

2100 hours

Eight of them stood, gathered around Jan's body. Moshe was crouched on the floor, checking for a pulse along the elderly man's neck. He turned toward the others.

"He's gone."

"Come on, help me," Elias urged the others. The rabbi, with the help of Berkovitz, dragged the body to the wall at the far end of the barrack. He positioned the body so that his feet faced the door. He then took one of Moshe's scraps of paper and placed it over Jan's face. He pulled one of the tattered blankets from the floor and laid it over the body.

"Poor Jan, what a miserable tallith to wear," he whispered.

Using his teeth, Elias tore a piece from the side of the cloth. After a moment's hesitation, Moshe, Berkovitz, Jiri, and Myriam each did the same. The others gathered together at the far end of the barrack, near the entrance.

"Would anyone like to say anything?" asked the rabbi.

The group looked around at one another.

"I didn't know him very well," Moshe began. "I believe he was a tailor, or something along those lines. What I can say is that I never knew him to be cruel to anyone. I never saw him push his way to the washroom, and when we lined up for soup, he was always one of the first in line; it didn't matter to him that the best pieces were at the bottom. If he knew he could help someone, he always did."

"The surest way to get yourself killed here at camp," Jacek whispered to Paul.

The two followed the ceremony from a distance, catching glimpses through the apertures between the uniforms that hung on the line above. Elias looked at Myriam. It would have been her turn to recite the Kaddish, but she shook her head in refusal. So Elias drew in a deep breath and began the prayer of mourning. The other Jewish prisoners crossed to the sink and tried to wash their hands in the slight trickle of water that dripped forth. They then gathered once again around the table.

But Jiri remained crouched on the floor. He had a bleary look about him: for despite having been at the camp for seven months, he had not yet been accustomed to death itself. He sprung to his feet. Closing his eyes, he bowed his head and began to sing. The song followed a rhythm that seemed to evoke the age-old melodies of the gypsies.

"What's he singing?" Berkovitz asked Moshe in a hushed tone.

"An *endecha*," he answered with a whisper.

"Sephardic funeral songs. Jiri is quite a piece of work."

The Pink Triangle sang with such consuming sadness that the others were unable to hold back their tears. At the close of his song, his final notes seemed to reverberate through the air for an instant before falling into the silence that shrouded each and every thing.

Jiri opened his eyes, as if waking from a trance, and asked: "Now what do we do?"

"There's still time. We have eleven hours left."

"Yes, but we're tired," Berkovitz said, "and hungry. And in a short while, we will be in no position to reason. I feel quite weak. All I want is to sleep."

"He's right," Moshe stated. "In a few hours, we'll hardly be able to speak. My throat is dry. I'm growing more and more tired. We need to decide now."

"Right, we do need to decide now." Jacek turned to look at Myriam, but Paul shot him a scathing glance.

"Listen," Berkovitz proposed, "we've got pencils and scraps of paper. There's no reason to continue to discuss anything. I say we cast a vote, each of us will be on our own. And at the end, we'll tally everything up."

"The only free vote in the Third Reich," quipped Moshe. He gathered the larger pieces of paper from the table and, along with pencils, he distributed them to the others. They then each retreated to a separate corner. One of the prisoners drifted to the dark corner of the room, keeping a distance, however, from Jan's body.

It didn't take very long. One by one they each dropped their folded scraps of paper onto the table.

"Berkovitz, you want to do it? Is it all right with everyone?" The others nodded.

The financier crossed to the table. He positioned his glasses squarely atop his nose; he reached for the first scrap of paper, unfolded it, and read it aloud.

"Alexey."

The Ukrainian grew pale.

Berkovitz returned the piece of paper to the table and picked up another.

"Alexey."

In a state of fury, the aide to the *Blockältester* lunged in the direction of Berkovitz. He tore the paper out of Berkovitz's hands in an effort to seize control, despite knowing his act was futile. At having seen his own name, he exploded into a stream of profanity, whose meanings were known to him alone; he then threw the crumpled piece of paper onto the floor.

Berkovitz had managed to keep a cool head about him. Without taking heed of the interruption, he reached for the third piece.

"Alexey."

"You pigs!" screamed the Ukrainian. "Dirty pigs. Bloody Jews!"

No one offered a response. Alexey retreated into a corner, enraged, livid, panting.

"There's nothing written on this one. It's blank," said Berkovitz.

"Did you ask for advice from your god only to find that he was out of the office, Elias?" Moshe asked.

"I told you. I will never condemn another to death by giving a name."

"Let's move on."

Berkovitz opened the squashed scrap of paper. His face drained of all color.

"Myriam."

Alexey was replete with joy. Paul bit his lip. Moshe, too, winced at the sound of the name.

"You mean to throw yourself to the wolves, Myriam?"

"I have no reason to live, you of all people should know that, Moshe."

Berkovitz continued to tally the polls with the impassivity of an administrative board.

"Alexey . . . Alexey . . . Jacek."

The others turned to the chief barrack leader, who offered only an air of indifference.

"Alexey."

And that was it.

Berkovitz picked up the scrap that Alexey had tossed and placed it with the others. He arranged them as best he could, stacking one atop the other, straightening the pile with the palm of his hand.

"Would anyone like to check?"

No one answered. In the corner, Alexey shook with suppressed rage.

"Well then, let's see . . Alexey six votes. Myriam and Jacek one vote and one blank ballot. Nine in all."

The room was silent. The others turned to Alexey, who was now foaming with anger.

"You worthless swine. You have an SS officer here and yet . . . you choose me! Spineless cowards to the very end! *Judenschweine!*"

No one dared move. Moshe spoke. "Alexey, Alexey, you must not have been very good at math then, am I right?"

"What do you mean?"

"You didn't add it up? You had six votes. But there are only five Jews here. One of whom voted a blank ballot and another who voted for herself. So what might you deduce now, Alexey?"

The criminal struggled to follow Moshe's explanation.

"What do you mean to say? Go ahead, just say it then!"

"Three Jews, three votes for you. As for the others, Alexey, who were they? Haven't you asked yourself this very question?"

The Kapo's aide scanned the room, disquieted by the sudden realization of a new danger that had been left unheeded, until now.

"There are still three other votes, Alexey. Think about it."

The rabid eyes of the Ukrainian were suddenly affixed upon Otto.

"Well done," Moshe remarked. "That wasn't so difficult. Two more."

Alexey eyed the others skeptically, but when his eyes fell upon Paul, he had no doubt.

"Excellent, you found the fifth vote. An SS officer. That's quite a kick in the pants, isn't it? Bet you hadn't expected that."

"You are the vile scum of mankind," Hauser said with bitter contempt. "You are worse than the Jews."

"Good then, just one more to go, Alexey," Moshe said encouragingly.

Alexey continued to scan the room, passing over each of the others.

And then, all of the sudden, he stopped. His eyes were emblazoned by a revelation that brought both shock and dismay.

"But, of course: Jacek. Who did you think?" exclaimed Moshe.

Alexey sputtered, unable to give an explanation. Jacek stood impassively at a safe distance.

"What did you think, that you would protect each other for all eternity?" Moshe carried on. "The truth being it's either you or him."

Alexey gnashed his teeth, plagued by the sudden disloyalty. The men looked on, their muscles taut, ready to intervene in the event of an attack. Only Myriam remained detached from the scene; her eyes seemed affixed to a point in the dark empty space. She gave no sign of interest in the impending brawl.

The others looked on in disbelief as Moshe crossed to Alexey, stopping with only a few paces in between them. He broke into a grin.

"Nevertheless, you can't complain."

"What do you mean? Say what you mean to say!"

"Oh, come on, Alexey! Who then do you think voted for Jacek?"

The only reaction from the Kapo came by way of a sneer.

"It's either you or him. Him or you. You're both well aware

of it. And now, you're even. You're not as stupid as you seem, Alexey."

The Ukrainian dodged his superior's stare. The wolf pack had been divided.

"What fine company we have, indeed!" trilled Jiri. From a crouched position he sprang into a graceful pirouette.

"Your friendship," he began, addressing both Jacek and Alexey, "moves me. It calls to mind an old Jewish folktale. Would you like to hear it?"

"It wouldn't be the one about the tailor, would it?" Moshe started in.

"There were two men who were the dearest of friends. One was a businessman and the other was a tailor. The businessman often went to his friend to have his suits tailored. During one of these visits, while trying on his own suit, he noticed that his friend's clothes were torn and tattered. 'Those are not clothes fit for a tailor!' he cried. And the other said, 'You are right, my friend. But I am not wealthy like you, and cannot afford to buy a new suit.' 'I see,' responded the other, 'then I shall give you two zloty so that you may repair your suit.' The other took the money and earnestly thanked his friend. Two weeks later, the businessman chanced upon the tailor and noticed that his suit was still the same tattered mess as before. Naturally, he was befuddled, and so he asked his friend to explain. The tailor shook his head and said, 'You know, you were quite right. The suit was intended to be quite awful. And had I repaired it with two miserable zloty, I really would have lost all my earnings!'"

Jiri waited for his audience's consent.

"Well, did you like it? It seems perfectly suited for the situation. Only that, I can't decide who would be the businessman and who would be the tailor. Jacek or Alexey? What do you all think?"

"Come on," Otto said, ignoring the inquiry. "Let's get this over with. We've made our decision. Let's finish this." With that he turned and shot a steadfast glance in Paul's direction and headed toward the Ukrainian. A few seconds passed and Jacek joined them.

Alexey stood squarely against the wall. From beneath his jacket, he unsheathed his knife.

"Stop! Take one step closer and I'll split out your guts. I'm going to kill at least one of you before they have me shot."

The three stopped at a safe distance, ready to spring into attack.

"Wait," Moshe ordered. "There's no need to get our hands dirty. Let the jackboots take care of it. Call the Oberscharführer."

But Moshe hadn't time to voice the rest. Falling prey to his own instincts, Alexey lunged at Paul. But the soldier, both healthy and strong, dodged the attack with ease. He spun around and struck a sharp blow with his fist to Alexey's wrist, so that the knife fell to the ground. With a swift kick, Jacek sent the knife sliding to the far end of the barrack.

Alexey collected himself, and stood with his fists raised, panting like a hunted animal. The three men circled him, preventing any effort to escape. For a moment, no one moved. It was just enough time for Alexey to weigh the remaining possibilities. And with that the lull was broken; suddenly Alexey hurled himself at Jacek, dealing a sharp blow to his face, and ran.

"Stop him!" Paul shouted, but Moshe, Berkovitz, and Jiri all stood motionless.

Alexey, followed by Otto and Paul, raced toward the door. He knew there would be not enough time to open it. In that instant, he changed course and headed for the window. With a blanket dragging behind him, which would shield him from the crash, Alexey hurled himself through the window amid the sound of breaking glass.

At the same moment, the others inside the barrack could hear furious shouts from the watchtower. Beams of blinding light advanced upon the barrack. And then Alexey was heard shouting. "Wait! Wait! It's Alexey, the barrack *Stubendienst*—"

A round of machine-gun fire unleashed, then another, and yet still another.

Silence.

Keeping close to the wall, Paul peered out of the shattered window.

"He's dead," he announced.

They could still hear the aggravated clamor of the guards when the door swung open; the Oberscharführer appeared, infuriated.

"What the hell happened?"

No one offered an answer. They stood with their eyes cast downward.

"The commander is going to have it out with me! I demand an explanation this instant."

"Herr Oberscharführer," Moshe began. "Alexey attempted to violate the commander's orders. We tried to stop him, but it was not possible."

The officer looked puzzled.

"What are you saying, Moshe?"

"The commander ordered that we choose one person here. We did that. We chose Alexey. He tried to escape. We were only obeying the orders of Herr Kommandant."

The warrant officer assessed Moshe's story with uncertainty.

"No one broke any rule, Herr Oberscharführer. Except for Alexey, of course. We were only following orders."

The SS lingered, still uncertain.

"I will relate this to the commander," he said after a lengthy silence. "Don't cause any more trouble, or it will only become worse for all of you."

Breitner, his wife, and little Felix were seated at the table that had been laid with fine Bohemian china over a solitary tablecloth of damask linen and lace. At the center of the table, a freshly uncorked bottle of Bordeaux had been placed. Behind them, dressed in a simple uniform with a starched cap, stood the maid. She was a young Jehovah's Witness, whom Breitner himself had chosen to work as both the cook and the nanny, for they were known to be excellent at rearing children. The girl approached the table to serve the soup.

Her hand trembled. The commander's presence frightened her. As she served the soup, a drop fell upon Breitner's pants. Frieda sprang to her feet, slapping the girl with her napkin.

"Idiot!"

The commander stared coldly at the girl.

"Leave the room. We'll do it ourselves."

Frieda had not yet served the first course when they heard the sound of the doorbell. She began to head in the direction of the door, but Breitner stopped her with a wave of his hand. "Leave it. It will be the same nuisance. Go ahead, start without me."

The commander excused himself from the dining room. An attendant waited at the door, who sprang into a salute.

"Oberscharführer Schmidt is outside, sir. He is asking to speak with you. Shall I let him in?"

"No, I'll go out. I could use a smoke anyhow."

Just outside the home, the warrant officer waited at attention. The gravel square was subtly lit by the light cast from the house.

"At ease, Schmidt, at ease," the commander said.

He pulled a packet of French cigarettes from his uniform pocket, placed one between his lips and offered one to the officer.

"Want one, Herr Schmidt?"

The other man awkwardly accepted.

"Thank you, Herr Kommandant."

Breitner lit his cigarette with an ornate gold lighter; he held out the flame for the officer.

"Well, Herr Schmidt, what's happening with the prisoners from Block Eleven?"

"One of them tried to escape the barrack, Herr Kommandant."

Breitner couldn't help but smile.

"I see, and who was it?" He quickly added, "No, wait, let me guess. . . ."

He strode back and forth while his subordinate remained stock-still.

Three steps in one direction and then he turned round and headed back again. The gravel crunched beneath the soles of his boots. At each turn, Breitner would stop and expel a thick stream of smoke. The embers from the cigarette glowed in the half-light of the square.

"Let's see who it might have been . . . certainly not the woman, nor the Communist, that's for sure. None of the Jews, assuredly, for they are far too cowardly—" Disrupting his own reasoning, he spun on his heels quickly, and pointing to the officer with his cigarette, gave his verdict.

"Alexey, the Ukrainian. It was him, wasn't it?"

The Oberscharführer was visibly shocked

"Yes, Herr Kommandant, it was him, Alexey."

Breitner flashed a contented smile. With his cigarette between his fingers, he gestured toward the warrant officer.

"Tell the story."

"Without warning, he threw himself out of the window of the barrack. He shouted something in protest, but the rules were clearly laid out, and the guards from the watchtowers—"

"Shot him," Breitner said. "Is that what happened?"

"That is precisely what happened, Herr Sturmbannführer. The others claim that he was trying to violate orders after having been selected for execution."

"Good, good," Breitner mumbled through a long slow drag of his cigarette.

The Oberscharführer waited in discomfort. He smoked nervously, hoping to counter his obvious unease. The commander abruptly turned to him.

"My dear Schmidt, we have lost another pawn. It was, however, foreseeable. In the game of chess, they are the first pieces to be sacrificed. But this makes the game more interesting, wouldn't you say?"

"Ehm, yes . . . of course, Herr Kommandant."

Breitner smoked in silence.

"Excuse me, Herr Sturmbannführer, . . . what are your orders?"

"My orders . . . ? Ah, yes." The commander tossed what was left of his cigarette onto the ground and flattened it with his boot. Schmidt quickly followed suit. "My orders are that everything should remain just as it was before."

"But . . . should we increase the number of guards? I wouldn't want the prisoners to attempt another—"

"No," the commander interjected. "They won't try it again, of this I'm sure. Only a foolish, insignificant pawn would attempt such a stupid act. Keep me informed of every development in detail. You are not to overlook anything. Send word of any and every particular that might be of interest to me."

"May I go, Herr Sturmbannführer?"

"Yes . . . no, not just yet. In your opinion, Herr Schmidt, who will they choose?"

The officer became uneasy.

"I . . . wouldn't know, Herr Kommandant."

"Come on, out with it, Herr Schmidt, you needn't give a full report. Just tell me, between you and me, who do think they'll choose to send before the firing squad?"

"In my opinion, Herr Kommandant, given that the aide to the Kapo is dead, there's little doubt: they'll choose the barrack leader, Jacek."

"So you say, Herr Schmidt?"

The warrant officer unwittingly stood with his chest out. He was terribly pleased that his superior had taken an interest in his opinion.

"Yes, I do believe that's the case."

"And Paul Hauser? Have you forgotten him?"

"If he's smart, he'll keep quiet. He is not obligated, by any means, to reveal his identity."

"Indeed."

Breitner cast a sidelong smile that disquieted the warrant officer. Schmidt deemed it best to stay quiet.

"You see, Herr Schmidt, it is often the case that what appear to be simple movements on a chess board are much more complex than what we might initially detect. A piece that seems destined for destruction, can in fact, be the very piece to place the king in check. You may go, Herr Oberscharführer."

The officer sprang to attention and stretched his arm in a taut salute. He turned, and before he could make much headway, the commander called his name.

"Herr Oberscharführer!"

The warrant officer turned on his heels.

"I've changed my mind," Breitner said. "Everything stays just as it was before, except for one thing. Inform the prisoners that I'm still awaiting a name. But now, they have less time at their disposal. Rather than 0800 I want it by 0600. Since there are now fewer candidates, it ought to make choosing a little easier."

The officer snapped to attention and went on his way.

Breitner entered the house once again and made his way back to the dining room. He took his usual seat at the table, placed his napkin atop his knee, and then reached for his spoon.

"Is something the matter, dear?"

Breitner gave a smile.

"Oh no," he said as he brought the spoon to his lips.

"Just the usual nonsense."

2200 Hours

The patrol commander returned after half an hour.

The sound of the door startled the prisoners; all but Paul, who remained indifferent to the noise.

Jacek rubbed his cheek where Alexey had struck him, leaving behind an enormous bruise. Everyone stood at attention.

The Oberscharführer eyed each of the prisoners. His sidelong smile frightened them.

"The commander has ordered that you are to remain here. He awaits one of your names."

None of the prisoners dared breathe.

"He wants to know which one of you is to be executed"—he paused, scanning the room, eyeing each prisoner one by one—"by six o'clock."

The *Häftlinge* stood immobile, petrified. Only Moshe dared to speak.

"But—"

"The Oberscharführer crept menacingly toward Moshe.

"Did you not hear, Moshe? By six, I said."

"Alexey is dead, we had chosen him."

"The commander has ordered that one of you must be shot tomorrow. Shot, you understand? By a commanded platoon as stated in the regulations. Alexey was killed during an attempted escape. That is now a separate case entirely."

He turned on his heel and exited the barrack. Moshe closed the door.

"And now," he said, "we start all over again."

"Shall we go play, Papa?"

"No, Felix. It's late. You need to go to bed."

"Papa! We didn't finish the game. I don't want all of the pieces to just stand there all night waiting for us. They'll get so tired . . ."

"They're just chess pieces, Felix."

"That's not true! They have names now!"

The little boy cast an imploring look at his mother. She patted his head and turned to his father.

"A few more minutes won't do any harm. Go ahead upstairs. I'll tidy up down here . . . when I'm finished I'll come and put Felix to bed."

The little boy sprang to his feet. Though he did not really like chess, it was as good an excuse as any to avoid bedtime.

"All right then. Come on, Felix!"

Father and son climbed the stairs, one behind the other, until they reached the last room of the dormered attic. Felix leapt from one step to the next with the heady excitement of a child beyond exhaustion.

"Are you sure you want to stay up, Felix?"

"Oh, but of course I do, Papa!"

The two took their places at either side of the chessboard.

"Whose turn is it, Papa?"

"It's yours, Felix."

The little boy took hold of his pawn and with it, jumped ahead three squares.

"You can't do that, Felix. The pawn only moves one square at a time."

"But mine is special, Papa. I trained him. At the barracks I made him jump over lots of hurdles, from morning until night. At first, he could only jump two squares, and then three. You know, I created a special corps: the High Jump pawns. They are the only ones who can even kill a knight."

Breitner smiled. "He's a pawn, Felix. One square at a time, in a forward direction. Besides, you don't need your High Jump pawn."

Felix studied the board. His exhaustion clouded his thoughts. He moved a piece at random. His father then promptly captured the pawn with his bishop. The little boy seemed puzzled.

"And there goes another," Breitner declared, "you have only eight to go."

"Now I'll beat you, Papa."

Breitner grinned. "We shall see."

"All right, who wants to begin?"

Moshe cast Otto an expectant glance, yet even the politician seemed depleted of energy; their exhaustion, hunger, and dehydration was quickly consuming them.

"Berkovitz?"

"We could take another vote."

"It would be somewhat useless, wouldn't it?" Moshe glimpsed about the room at the others. Jiri looked away, offering no counsel. Myriam, sat silently in a corner, lost in thought.

"And if we refused to choose a name?" Elias asked.

"What do you mean?"

"Tomorrow morning, when our last hour comes to an end, we will tell the commander that we have not chosen any name. We leave it in the hands of God."

Berkovitz struggled to grasp Elias's proposal.

"What do we gain from that? All eight of us will die."

"Don't you see? We are already condemned. We have already been given our sentence. All of us. Even you," he contended, directing his words at Paul, "even you, yes, even the son of a major general. The Russians are but a few fifty miles from here. And soon, your mighty Reich will be obliterated. Do you think that Berlin is troubled by your welfare? What delusions you must have to think that your father protects you; you haven't even the assurance that the man is alive."

The SS shivered with agitation, but offered no response. Yet the allegations had clearly hit home.

"Breitner could simply report that you were killed in an accident, that you were violently attacked by a dirty Jew even. Breitner tried to intervene, but it was too late. There are thousands of ways to die here at camp. The incinerator is but one."

"We don't know if Breitner intends to kill all of us or not," Berkovitz insisted. "We don't have all of the facts."

"We'll die either way, either here or at the *kremchy*," Elias said. "But if we refuse to provide Breitner a name, it will be our victory, and he will have lost. We will not have yielded to his threats. And in that way, even armed with his guards and machine guns, we will be more powerful. He can send us to the incinerators, but he cannot force us to condemn our fellow man."

Moshe moved toward the man whose wife he loved, his mouth curved by a habitual ironic smile.

"We have the possibility of sacrificing one life so that seven others may be spared. Does it seem inconsequential to you? Remember that Abraham was willing to sacrifice Isaac. We are fortunate that we are not forced to sacrifice a child, but rather a mere tyrant."

Moshe looked upon Jacek, who coldly returned his stare.

Berkovitz nodded. Otto, too, gave a nod of approval.

"Alexey's death offered us no reprieve," Moshe said. "And now . . ."

"And now I am all that is left." Jacek said, undaunted.

"I think the others would agree."

"I do," Otto said without hesitation.

"Yes, as do I," Berkovitz concurred.

"Jiri?"

"Need you even ask? Take a look at this." He rolled up the legs of his pants all the way to his groin. His thigh was an immense mass of black and blue. "Do you remember this, Jacek? If Alexey was tired or busy, you were there to bludgeon us to please the jackboots."

"Elias, you don't want to choose, we already know. Paul?"

The German gave a shrug. "It's okay by me."

"We're missing Myriam," observed Berkovitz.

The woman lifted her head and looked toward the others.

"I don't know Jacek. I don't know anything about him. So, I can't say. I know only this: I know that he wants to live. And I don't."

"Myriam——" Moshe called to her, but she didn't let him finish.

"Moshe," she broke in. "You're forever seeking the role of the intermediary, aren't you? It's your livelihood. Now look." She pointed to the others, one at a time, beginning with Berkovitz. "He lives for his wealth. Otto for his revolution. Paul for his Führer, Elias for his God, Jiri for his art. And you, Moshe . . ."

She drew near to him. With her hand, she caressed his cheek.

Her voice softened. "You want to live because you love life. You find it all to be so magnificent. Even here, within these walls, you haven't lost this joy, have you?"

Moshe cast his gaze downward.

"All of you have tremendous reasons to carry on. There is a greater force within you that continues to sustain you, that gives you strength." Her eyes drifted. "I lived only for Ida. I don't believe in God." Elias cringed in distress, "Not anymore. I don't believe in money or the revolution. And I think that the Führer is nothing but a sad, pathetic little man. Call the commander and tell him that I am the one you have chosen. I haven't the courage to end it myself, to die from the fatal shock of the electric fence like so many others . . . so, instead . . ."

No one spoke.

Elias, Moshe, Jiri, and Berkovitz exchanged discomfited glances.

"No, Myriam," Moshe protested. "We won't."

Jacek shifted away from the spot he had occupied since they had arrived—his back squarely against the wall—and began to pace about the room. His arms were crossed over his chest, as if in an effort to shield himself.

"That leaves only me then."

"What did you expect? That we would be grateful for every time that you chose to beat us, or for every time that you had us beaten?" Otto labored to constrain his rage.

"I beat you, it's true."

"You used your club every chance you had."

Jacek drew in close to the Red.

"That isn't true, Otto. And you know it."

"You—"

"I hit you only when I knew it was necessary. When there was nothing else I could do."

"Something that occurred often enough. Enough, Jacek," Moshe interjected. "It will do you little good to feign the role of victim in our company. And don't tell us that you were obliged to do it; no one forced you to become a *Blockältester*. Many others refused it."

"That's true. No one forced me."

"The jackboots gave you extra rations; grease for your shoes, a slice of bread, a little margarine, perhaps a cigarette from time to time. You weren't made to work, you stayed out of the heat, you were exonerated from the selections. Yet, you did it only to survive, of course."

"Just like all of you. You all want to live."

"But not at this price. Not like this. If there is anyone here who deserves to die, it is you."

"I did it for bread and soup, that's true. But it isn't that simple." Berkovitz looked squarely at Jacek. "What do you mean?"

"Jiri told you that I was once a footballer. I played defense; I blocked goals. When you play, you respect the rules; otherwise, the referee blows the whistle and you're out of the game."

"Here they'd shoot you," Moshe said.

"There are rules here, too. And I respect those rules just as I would on the field. But, not always. When I played, there were opportunities—albeit rarely—to break those rules. It might have come when you realized that the ref's line of sight was obstructed by another player, and so you repositioned the ball with your hands. Or it might have been that you pretended the ball was still in, when it had, in fact, gone out. You might have fallen and feigned being fouled. There are instances in which you can cheat the ref, and when those moments presented themselves, I seized them."

"Not to worry," Moshe retorted, "We won't report you to the football federation."

"Everything is a parody for you—everything is said in jest, Moshe, but I'm talking about a serious matter. It's true that I'm a *Blockältester,* and it's true that I hit you in order to spare my own life—"

"Have you forgotten the rations of soup that you stole from the Muslims, the bread that wasn't given, and of the times you aided the SS with their selections?"

"See, exactly my point, Moshe. I did help them with the selections, you're right. And do you remember Karl, the cobbler?"

Moshe's expression darkened.

"I see that you do. Do you recall who had him placed in the *Kommando* workshops, where he was sheltered from the cold, rather than forcing him to unload quintals of railroad ties in temperatures ten below zero? And do you know why I did it, Moshe? Because I knew he would not have survived otherwise. I was faced with that decision, and I chose to send someone who could have withstood the elements. It was in an effort to help him."

"Give us another, Jacek."

"All right then, Moshe. Let me entertain your request. Do you remember the selections back in March, Moshe? Do you all remember them?"

No one could have forgotten them.

"Tell me, Moshe, what did I ask you to procure for me from Kanada?"

"Foundation, I believe."

"The kind that women wear, correct?"

"Yes, I believe so."

"And do you know what I did? Do you remember? I used it to color the *Häftlinge*'s pallid cheeks so that they would pass the selections. 'Run!' I told them when they were forced to lineup up for the medic, 'Run as if the devil himself were at your heels!' And thanks to that counsel and to the foundation, someone's life was spared."

"And many others' lives were not."

Jacek loomed inches from Moshe's face.

"Do you want another name, Moshe? Yours, Moshe. When you lay dying of dysentery two months ago, who managed to secure you a place at the Ka-Be? Tell me, who?"

"I would have managed on my own anyway."

"And who warned you of the selection that morning at the hospital? Who told you to return, at once, to the barrack? Who, Moshe?"

Around the table, there was only silence.

"I beat you, it's true. But there was nothing else I could have done. Had I not, they would have brought in another barrack leader, far more brutal than myself. Alexey perhaps. I beat you only when there was no alternative, severely enough to appease the SS officers but never with enough force to cause you any harm. And you, Jiri?"

The actor was startled.

"Earlier, you showed us your bruise. But had I not been the one to hit you, what would that SS officer who stopped you have done?"

Jiri shuddered. He gave no answer.

"He didn't like you, Jiri. You knew that. He hated you. What did he call you? Homosexual swine . . . and three weeks ago, he found you at *Appellplatz*. You were alone. He stopped you. He took your cap. And then, what did he do?"

"He threw it," the actor murmured in a feeble voice.

"Exactly right. He launched it over the line of guards. And what did he say? Go and pick it up! It was an order from an SS officer; you would have been forced to comply. Either you went and picked up the cap, in which case the guards would have fired and you would have become yet another prisoner killed during an attempted escape, or you disobeyed his command, in which case you would have been shot and killed by the SS officer himself. Am I right, Jiri?"

"Yes, you're right."

"In that moment, I passed by, and what did I do, Jiri? I pretended to have been looking for you. I grabbed you and beat you. The SS officer laughed and insisted I hit you harder yet. And then he left, content with his affairs and relieved of his rage. Had I not found you there, Jiri, where would you be now?"

Jiri's eyes were downcast. He didn't answer.

"The truth is that here at camp, you can either do as Elias and accept the trials and tests that God sends you, whatever they may be . . . or, you strategize. And strategizing isn't easy. Within these walls, it's all the more challenging. There is little space in which one can maneuver the field. You have five or six adversaries at any given moment. But the space is there. And I have used it when I could, in any capacity that I could, even if it meant risking my own life. If the jackboots ever learned of it, what do you think would happen to me? Would any of you possess the same courage?"

The others found no words. Otto walked the floor, pacing nervously back and forth. His mouth opened and then closed again without a sound. The silence was complete.

After a moment, he continued, "I ended up here because of my dealings in the black market, you know. You had to be fearless to survive in that business. But I had to do it. For my brother, Tadeusz."

"You've never spoken of your brother," Elias said.

"We were left on our own. My father died in the Great War, my mother not long after—from tuberculosis. Tadeusz worked in the rail yards, but I earned enough for the both of us, so I had always helped him. One night, one of the workers failed to move the rail switch, the train came on the wrong track, and my brother ended up underneath it. He lost an arm and a leg, and in turn, he lost his job. He can't move around on his own. In Warsaw, our house is on the fifth floor and because of his state, he's forced to stay at home all day."

With those words, Jiri's body stiffened. He gazed at Jacek with a surprised expression, as if he had come across an object he had lost long ago, only to discover it at the bottom of an old box. He started to say something, but then held back. The barrack leader carried on, unaware of Jiri's sudden anxious state.

"Do you see why I must survive at any cost? And why it was that I accepted the position of *Blockältester*? It was for him. If I were to die, he would no longer know what to do. No one would be there to help him. When they brought me here, I swore that I would leave here alive, at any cost."

Moshe exchanged glances first with Berkovitz, then Elias, and then Jiri.

"It looks like no one in here is guilty of anything," he said.

"Did you see, Papa?"

The little boy's eyes, heavy with sleep, suddenly opened wide.

"You were going to eat my bishop!" exclaimed Felix. "But instead, I got away."

Breitner gently caressed his son's head.

"Well done, Felix. You're becoming quite the player."

2300 Hours

"Enough with the talk. We mustn't delay."

Otto's vigor had returned. "I cannot wait any longer, my comrades need me."

Berkovitz lifted his glasses from his nose and rubbed his reddened eyes. "I haven't any other idea, but I've the impression—"

"That what?" Otto said.

"I do not believe that the commander chose us at random. He wanted to organize an experiment of sorts. Mengele enjoyed physical torture; for Breitner the appeal lies in the breaking point of the mental state. A rich Jew, a real estate agent, a rabbi, his wife, a criminal, an athlete, an elderly man, a financier, and even a former SS officer. . . . Don't you see? It is a scale reproduction of the camp. I have a feeling Breitner is enjoying himself tremendously. We are like laboratory rats looking in vain for a way out of the labyrinth."

"But I do know the way out," Otto said.

"Are you sure of that?" Berkovitz asked. "What if even your escape has become a component in Breitner's plan? Perhaps he already knows everything, and he's waiting out there for you. Perhaps he is simply dangling the bait; beneath the cheese there's bound to be a trap."

Otto bit his lip. A sudden look of doubt flashed across his face.

"This isn't helping us solve our problem," Moshe said. "Who do we choose?"

"Why not him?" Jacek asked in his cold tone.

The others turned with a shock to face the prisoner whom the *Blockältester* now indicted.

"Jiri? But why?"

Jiri, who had been crouched on the floor, stood up.

"Here I am. I'm ready. Sacrifice me upon the altar. I will be your lamb, as white as milk, as pure and chaste as an angel."

"Quiet, Jiri. Why him exactly, Jacek?"

"Come on, you know. No one is innocent here. Moshe, you do business with the jackboots. I obey their orders. And Jiri . . . he concedes to any and everyone, from the *Lagerkapos* to the SS."

The actor crossed the room toward Jacek with slow, undulating movements.

"Come now, darling. Don't make me jealous."

"Try to be serious for once," Jacek warned. "We all know how you managed to avoid work shifts and how it is that you've come by all of that extra margarine that you eat."

"I sing. I sing! Had you not heard, Jacek? The officers adore my melodies. *Ich bin die fesche Lola.*"

His harmonious falsetto timbre spread throughout the barrack, dispelling their anxieties. All of the prisoners stopped to listen to the melody that, for an instant, removed them from the hostile reality they now faced. Within those walls, one only needed to hear a few notes of music or a few lines of poetry to return to a world they had left behind.

"And then?" Jacek broke in. "After you've sung, what do you do?"

Jiri abruptly stopped his song, as if someone from the audience had hurled an insult upon his stage.

"Afterward," he said in a voice distorted with emotion. "Afterward." His tone had changed, as if his microphone had unexpectedly shut off; his voice returned to the customary timbre he assumed when speaking. "So, I'm the camp's whore. You're right. I've been with everyone at this camp, in exchange for a little extra *wassersuppe*. Moshe, you excel at business affairs. I don't. Money slips right through my fingers. Just look at me."

He flung his arms open theatrically.

"I'm small, and thin, and I haven't a muscle to my name. How long would I have lasted here before becoming a Muslim? I want to survive just as all of you do. Each of us must employ our own resources. As Myriam told us, you love life, Moshe. As do I. Immensely. But I am weak. I need someone there to help me. I've always needed help, even before, when I worked at the *kabarett*. I came to know all sorts of people, even SS officers—their freshly starched uniforms, their military gait, and that wild fury that animated them—our glorious Reich! Blond and blue-eyed, with bulging pectorals . . . they were gorgeous. Gorgeous and terribly dangerous. Don't think that it was easy."

His expression darkened.

"Once . . . once I was with an Oberscharführer. We were stretched out, naked in bed together, and we were eating. He had champagne brought to our room—who knows how he procured such a thing—and pâté de foie. Ah, what splendor. But at a certain point—"

Jiri was unable to continue. He shook. Myriam wrapped her arms around him, and after a moment, he seemed to have mustered the strength to start again.

"At a certain point, he took his pistol from his holster, and dipped the barrel of the gun into the pâté, as if it were a breadstick. He turned it around two or three times, resolutely. I watched without understanding. He had a strange smile on his face. Then, he ordered me to turn around, so that I faced away from the dirty barrel of the gun. I pleaded but . . . there was nothing else I could do. He seemed to have lost his mind. He kept shouting 'dirty homosexual pig,' 'faggot Jew.' And so I obeyed. I laid down, my stomach to the sheets. He tied me to the bed, and then, with his pistol he"—his voice broke—"he sodomized me. He climbed on top of me and shoved the barrel inside of me. He was all over me. I couldn't turn around, but I could feel his breath on my neck and his body against my own. 'And now, you Jewish pig, do you know what I'm going to do?' he asked me, snickering in my ear. I was terrorized, I couldn't move; I was frightened to death, and yes, at a certain point, I shat myself. When he realized what had happened, he lost control. He screamed and I cried and pleaded with him while the stench penetrated everything around us. 'Filthy Jewish pig, now you're going to die!' he screamed. 'Now, I'll shoot you, I'll shoot you!' he shouted just as I felt the barrel inside of me again. And then . . . he pulled the trigger. I heard the click of the hammer, and for a moment, I thought I was dead. But the chamber was empty. I don't know if he meant for it to happen that way, or if I was just lucky. And just like that, without another word, he lay on the bed, his stomach to the ceiling. He seemed beside himself. I think I must have passed out; when I came to, he had left. I was still tied to the bed. I had to wait until the following day, before anyone found me there, in a puddle of blood and shit."

No one dared utter a word. The images of that brutal scene seemed to hang heavily in the air.

"But, luckily, they weren't all that way," Jiri said with a smile.

"I've passed more inspections than a general! I always thought they would help me survive. A Jew who tells jokes isn't a threat, he's just a Jew. But a Jew you take to bed, isn't a Jew anymore, right? No, he's a lover, a friend, a companion. How foolish . . ."

Moshe lowered his eyes, embarrassed. Paul watched content-edly.

Jiri's tone changed; his voice was now filled with aggression.

"I used my body, it's true. And for this I have no regrets; this is true too. But, at the very least, I can attest to never having used anyone else but my own self. Not everyone here can say the same for themselves."

The Pink Triangle glared ostentatiously in the direction of Berkovitz.

"Moshe might do business with the jackboots, but in the end, it's a survival tactic. And in truth, he's helped all of us too: thanks to him we've been lucky enough to come by things that are all but prohibited here. Yet you, Berkovitz, you've never restricted yourself to a few cigarettes or a new shirt. You contracted work with the Nazis. You loaned money to Krupp, Thyssen, Flick, Schaeffer, and who knows who else—their intentions mattered little to you, be it Hitler, the Nazis, the armies they were amass-ing, or the Jews that they intended to annihilate—your only con-cern was money. You believed that money would be your saving grace, because, in the end, money is neither Aryan nor Jew. Yet, by the time you figured out that they would offer you no re-prieve, it was altogether too late. They cheated you simply so that they could embezzle more for themselves in the end."

Berkovitz's jaw was pulled taut. The frames of his glasses glim-mered. His body had become rigid. "I wasn't the only one who was willing to sort their affairs. All of Europe—"

"But you're a *Jew*, Berkovitz!" Jiri interrupted him, "Don't forget that. You are a Jew. Had they not told you what the Nazis intended to do with us?"

"They told us of all sorts of conspiracies, but no one knew for sure. Finances were my trade; for that, I am not to blame."

"And yet, I'd say you are more to blame than all the rest,"

Jiri said in a sudden deep timbre. "You betrayed your own brothers."

"I—"

Before Berkovitz could finish, Elias intervened.

"Jiri is right. You knew what was happening in the rest of Europe, and feigned ignorance. You carried on your affairs even as the first truckloads of prisoners were being carried off. You supplanted God with money."

Berkovitz stood trembling; his self-assured façade of power had vanished.

"You're not the only one, however." Elias continued. "They say that even in Budapest, the wealthiest Jews are buying their safety, and to hell with everyone else. They say that in Switzerland they're preparing to send train cars laden with riches to the Nazi chiefs. God sought to test us, but not all have been worthy of his challenge."

Paul remained in his corner, silent. A faint smile spread across his lips. It took little effort to imagine what a Nazi thought of their quarrels.

"You're right. All of you," Berkovitz admitted. "I thought that money would have spared myself, my family, and for that matter, many of us. Money is a powerful tool; it can buy most anyone. But they didn't take everything from me. I managed to secure a vast amount in Switzerland; in Zurich I have millions upon millions in gold. As long as we survive here, in some way or another . . . after that, we needn't worry about anything. We can use the gold to sway the commander even. The jewels in Kanada are rubbish by comparison. I have friends in Poland who have already begun their operations. They'll find a way to get us out of here. They'll send us to another camp, one from which it is easier to escape. We'll find a way, you'll see. Stick with me, we'll survive together."

"Are you trying to buy us, Berkovitz?" Moshe asked in a cold voice.

"No, I—"

"It certainly seems that way. We're here, stuck in this damned barrack, our own prisoners, being forced to choose who we will sacrifice. And out of nowhere, you bring up this notion of money. All right, Berkovitz: take out your checkbook; it's payday."

Moshe, Jiri, Elias, and Otto eyed the financier with an air of disapproval. Paul, alongside Jacek, kept a safe distance; the barrack leader seemed consumed by his own calculations.

Myriam moved in closer. Placing her hand on Berkovitz's chest, a gesture that seemed, at once, both a caress and a forceful shove in the opposite direction.

"He isn't to blame for this," she said, turning toward the others. "It is the fault of the times in which we now live. All of us here, every one of us, even him," she said, pointing toward Paul, "we are all being destroyed by something much greater than us. No one is to blame." She turned to her husband. "Weren't you the one, Elias, who always told me, 'Better to suffer than to be cause of injustice'?"

Husband and wife looked at each other.

"No, Myriam," Moshe said. "Our faults are not each the same. You've either resisted or conceded. You've either ignited insult or have been forced to defend yourself from it."

The others, exhausted, tried to get some rest. Jiri laid upon the floor; the others were either sprawled across the heap of linens or splayed about on the wooden floor with a blanket beneath them.

"I think—" Moshe began, though his sentence was abruptly interrupted by the ear-splitting howls of the sirens that suddenly thundered through the camp.

"We're being bombed!" Moshe cried.

Felix had fallen asleep; his head lay atop his folded arm. Breitner softly caressed the little boy's blond head while he continued to study the chessboard.

"You see, Felix," he explained, though the child could not hear him, "this is what happens when there isn't any discipline."

He pointed to the eight remaining white pieces.

"Just when it seems that the enemy will triumph, panic ensues. Every man looks to save only himself, and in doing so, they open the door to defeat. Yet, if they were simply to band together, they might withstand the enemy's attacks, or at the least, lessen their losses."

The door opened and Frieda entered. When she saw that the little boy had fallen asleep, a tender smile spread across her face.

"I'll put him to bed," she spoke in a soft tone.

"I'll help you," Breitner answered.

In that instant, the alarms began to sound. The commander drew the child close to him, an instinctive, protective gesture. Frieda looked at her husband, her eyes filled with fright.

"Don't worry, I don't think they're headed here," Breitner reassured her.

The noise woke Felix. He opened his eyes, still laden with sleep.

"Papa." He remembered the game. He lowered his eyes toward the board. "The pawns . . ."

"We'll finish it tomorrow, don't worry. But right now I'm taking you to bed."

The sound of the alarms grew ever more piercing. Breitner cupped his hands over the little boy's ears.

"You needn't be afraid," he whispered. "It's nothing. It will all be over shortly. Now, get some sleep."

2400 Hours

Inside the barrack, the prisoners shouted with joy.

"They're coming, they're coming! You sorry jackboots, bet even you're afraid now, aren't you?"

Jiri broke into another falsetto rendition of "*Ich bin die fesche Lola,*" swishing about the barrack as if he found himself upon a vast stage. Moshe grabbed hold of his hands, and together, the pair danced for a few comical turns across the wooden floor that creaked with every step.

"Come on!" cried Otto. "Come and finish everyone off, blow everything away! Long live Stalin! Long live Lenin! Long live the party!"

"Long live Churchill!" Moshe shouted.

Elias pushed aside the linens that had blocked the window and peered out at the sky. He scoured the darkness for a glimpse of the planes overhead. Even Myriam seemed overcome with a strange excitement.

"Drop the bombs! Drop them and finish if off!" Moshe implored.

After a few minutes, their euphoria dwindled. The rumble of

the aircrafts moved farther away as the noise of the alarm sirens diminished in intensity.

"But where are they going?" Otto cried. The politician leaned as if to peer out of the window.

"Be careful," Moshe warned. "The jackboots are in a panicked state out there, they're all too eager to fire a shot."

"They're leaving," Elias observed.

"Come back!" Otto cried.

"Today wasn't the day," Moshe replied, unable to conceal his disappointment.

"They're headed for Silesia," Paul informed them as he removed himself from the corner. "Lucky for us," he added. "You're all mad. If they were going to bomb the crematoriums, they would have hit the camp as well. Do you not see what would have happened?"

A feverish smile flashed across Moshe's face.

"*Nu?* They would have destroyed the crematoriums. As for the rest, who gives a damn!"

"Who gives a damn!" Tiri repeated. "To hell with the jackboots and all of their iron crosses!"

"And yet, they've gone after another target," contested Paul. "They don't give a damn about you. I am military, and I know how the military reason. Everyone, both here and in the nearby posts, are just Communists, Social Nationalists, and capitalists. Their objective is to strike developmental posts. Without armies, there is no war. Without armies, the enemy cannot kill you. In order to reach this camp, the bomber pilots must cover twelve hundred miles of enemy territory. Do you suppose they would risk an entire fleet of aircrew to save a handful of civilians?"

"Tens of thousands of civilians," Moshe answered.

"For the military, a civilian is only an impediment in their operation. There's only you and the enemy. All of the rest is *Scheiße*."

His words held heavy resonance; their excitement vanished as quickly as it had arrived.

"Don't you get it?" the German continued. "The Anglo-Americans don't care whether a few Jews end up being exterminated. When it's all said and done, they might even be in favor of it."

The alarms ceased.

The sudden silence was almost deafening. Only a few orders were discharged to the guards together with the baying of frightened dogs. And then, nothing.

"It's over," Berkovitz said. "They're not coming back. They're not going to bomb this place."

"But don't they know?" Elias asked. "Don't they know that they're planning to occupy Hungary?"

"The jackboots told me that, in a few months, they expect a million detainees."

"Then they'll start the selections again."

"But isn't anyone going to do anything?" Jiri said, horror-struck.

"They must be stopped! The Pope."

"The Pope himself is praying," answered Elias.

"That they annihilate us all, perhaps," Moshe resounded.

They surrendered to their fatigue once again. With wearied hands, Moshe and Elias repositioned the linens over the shattered window to better block the cold draft. They then took a seat on the floor, one next to the other, with their backs to the wall. Jiri made his way to Myriam at the far end of the room. She shifted slightly, in an effort to make room, and Jiri nestled in next to her. Paul and Otto were seated at the table, beneath the light, facing each other. Berkovitz, followed by Jacek, moved to the back of the room. With a sigh of relief, they each stretched out atop a heap of blankets, taking care to stay far away not only from Jiri and Myriam, but also from Jan's body. The prisoners drifted in and out of sleep: unable to rest and yet far too fatigued to remain alert.

A heavy silence fell upon them.

Breitner carried the little boy, who remained fast asleep, to bed. He envied the innocent, peaceful sleep of children. For a moment, he felt as if he were back in the workshops in Munich; every now and then, they would ask him to lend a hand moving the boxes and shelves. At the foundry, the trucks would unload slabs of iron measuring half a foot in length, which would later ship out in the form of screws, bolts, wrenches, and washers. Raw material would arrive and the finished product would later go out. Within the camp, their work was very much the same: but the production line worked in the opposite order: men would arrive; ashes would later be all that remained.

He returned to the dormered study. He peered out the window that gave way to the entire camp, a view now immersed in darkness. Thousands of men who threatened the Reich's integrity were being exterminated; there was no other choice. But, first, their labor needed to be utilized to the fullest extent. The prisoners needn't suffer too much, but they needn't prosper either. A thought sprang to mind; he grabbed the telephone and dialed a number.

"Hello, Herr Oberscharführer?"

"*Jawohl, mein Offizier!*" The voice on the other end of the line emitted a metallic and distant echo, a sound that agitated the commander.

"Any news from the prisoner's barrack?"

"After the attempted escape, none, *mein Herr.*"

"Was soup supplied to them?"

Breitner detected a faltering sigh from the other end of the line.

"No, Commander, sir. Your orders . . ." The warrant officer was unable to finish.

"Did I order them to die of hunger, then, Herr Oberscharführer?"

"No, Commander, sir. But . . ."

"The rules clearly state that in the absence of specific command you are to proceed with standard protocol, or had you forgotten?"

"I . . ."

"The soup must be supplied twice a day to all prisoners, a practice only to be revoked if they are dead! Are you to inform me that all of those prisoners are dead, Herr Oberscharführer?"

"No, Herr Kommandant."

"Then see it to it immediately!"

The commander hung up the receiver before a response could be voiced from the other end. In an effort to calm himself, he interlaced his fingers, one hand crossing into the other; he turned his palms outward and extended his arms in a stretch. But with no relief from his apprehension, he began to wonder as to precisely what was troubling him so.

0100 Hours

"You've little time left. This war will soon end," Otto said, looking squarely at Paul, who was seated across the table. His voice was low; he was exhausted, but did not want to succumb to his fatigue. Morning was approaching too quickly.

"They're studying the other armies in Berlin," the officer retorted. "They'll bomb London with V-2s. They'll raze it to the ground. They've got heavy water too. There's no escape. Next year they'll initiate a counteroffensive in the east. And by Christmas, we'll invade Moscow."

"Napoleon said the same thing."

"Napoleon didn't have V-2s."

"Come on, Paul, you know that, sooner or later, the Russians will hit Berlin and it will be all over for Hitler."

"But, Otto . . . you're German. I can't understand how the collapse of our motherland would make you happy."

The Red bore a slight grimace.

"I don't know . . . it's true. It's not easy to choose. I love Germany, but I hate Hitler. He's a maniac." Otto looked squarely at Hauser. "I'm convinced you think the same thing."

"We don't choose our leaders."

"That isn't so; you could appeal the ruling."

"In the military you follow orders."

"You went against orders once before. Because, in truth, you too are fighting for ideals, though they are flawed. Tremendously flawed. But you haven't waged this war for yourself. You fight because you believe in the promise of a better future, even if that future does not coincide with my own."

"And what about you?"

"My ideals differ greatly from your own."

"What, those of Communism? You really believe that? Your leaders steal just as our generals do. There are times when I see no difference between you and us. Stalin is just as maniacal as Hitler. Tell me that isn't true."

Otto started to reply, but fell silent.

"Can you tell me the difference between your working class and my *Volk*? Very little, it would seem. . . ."

They sat in silence, each analyzing the other.

"What trade were you in before you entered the SS?"

Paul gave a defiant huff.

"I left home when I was eighteen. I didn't get on very well with my father."

"The major general?"

"From the time I was very small, his sole objective was to teach me discipline, order, and rules. When I was six years old, he had me bathing in freezing water at five thirty in the morning. Afterward, it was off to the woods where I was to march for two or three hours. Once, I almost died from pneumonia."

"And your mother?"

"My mother was terrified. He always hit me. He whipped me. And she . . . she never did anything. She never said anything. And I hated her for that."

All at once, Paul's eyes, which habitually bore a look of inso-

lence, were filled with sadness. His old wounds seemed to have
suddenly reopened.

"But then, why did you enlist?"

"Tell me, Otto, did you ever look at the big picture? We
loathe our own parents, we curse them and swear never to be
like them . . . and yet, in the end, we make their very same mis-
takes."

"And so, you became an SS."

"My father is in the Wehrmacht. They detest the SS. They
consider us unreliable, without discipline, and moreover to be
politically corrupt and having no respect for military tradition.
To tell you the truth, Otto, I suppose I became an SS officer to
spite my own father."

"You obviously didn't succeed, given that he's intervened in
order to protect you."

"He has his own way of showing that he cares. Though he
might have spared my life in hopes of teaching me a lesson. We'll
never understand each other."

"At least you have a father."

"Otto, tell me, have you always thought only of the party?"

"Have you always thought only of the Führer?"

"Of course not. I enjoy many things."

"Women?"

"Bikes. They're a vice of mine."

Otto's eyes lit up. "Bikes? Which bikes?"

"A Zündapp KS750. You know it?"

"Two-cylinder four-stroke engine," Otto recited. "With a
compression of six point two to one, maximum twenty-four
horsepower at six thousand RPM, an overhead valve distribution,
a Solex BFRH thirty carburetor, and a reservoir of six gallons.
Max speed is sixty miles an hour. She's magnificent."

"Have you driven one?"

"Once. A comrade in my division owned one. But I'd argue the BMW R75 is better."

"You've got to be joking. It isn't half as powerful as the Zündapp."

"The BMW has a Graetzin twenty-four carburetor. It's in an entirely separate class from the Solex."

"I see you've never owned one. And the frame? That BMW is pressed steel; it's hardly as . . ."

"Well, look at that," Moshe quietly said to Elias, who was seated on the floor next to him. The coarse wooden floorboards were marked with vast damp stains. He pointed toward both Paul and Otto, who were engrossed in conversation. "A moment ago they were at each other's throats, and now it seems as if—"

"Just like Moses and Aaron. Couldn't have been more different. And yet, they managed to get along."

"Ah, the Germans. At any rate, between Hitler and Stalin, I'm not sure who's worse. The Russians have yet to bring their war with the Nazis to a close, and yet they've already begun to fight the Americans. I liked the world as it was before. Do you remember Warsaw before the war? It was a beautiful place. Now, I fear, all of that will change."

"Those who fear the future have lost their childhood spirit."

"You're right, Elias. I no longer have the spirit of my childhood. Though, I never did. Do you know that I hated you?"

Taken aback, Elias looked up to meet Moshe's gaze.

"You . . . hated me?"

"For what you had done to Ida. I never believed that you had the right to do what you did. Not even a father has the right to sacrifice their own child. Not even you."

Elias stared at Moshe, shocked by his words.

"Myriam hated you, too," Moshe continued. "It wasn't love

that brought about the affair. It was hatred. We both meant to hurt you, and we sought the most painful means."

Elias laid his head on the blanket spread upon the floor and closed his eyes.

"I'm sorry," Moshe said. "But that's the way it was when we were in the ghetto."

The two remained silent.

"And now?" Elias asked after a moment had passed.

"Now I'm even more convinced: no one has the right to sacrifice the life of another human being. Ever."

Elias heaved a sigh.

"You see, you agree with me." Elias kept his eyes away from Moshe. "I too have learned from all of this. And for that reason, I have no intention of yielding to their absurd requests. You erred in a way that I know I can never forgive you for. But in doing so, you opened my eyes. I deserved to be punished for what I had done. Perhaps God had chosen that path for us."

"God had nothing to do with it, Elias."

"God has everything to do with it. Even here, in this moment, when it seems as if he has forgotten us. You betrayed your own friend. But I . . ." He sighed once more. He stared at Moshe, his eyes wide with guilt. "I betrayed my own child. Your fault is far less grave."

Moshe sat, troubled, with restless hands.

"Perhaps our efforts would have been futile; perhaps we would not have been able to help her escape in the end. Or perhaps she was saved just the same."

Elias slowly shook his head. "This does not amend what either I or you have done. It is up to God to judge us, or perhaps, to forgive us."

Elias struggled to his feet and then, bending his legs, he kneeled upon the floor. From the recesses of his uniform, he pulled out a ragged piece of cloth. He placed it on his head. He then leaned forward so that his forehead touched the floor.

"Go away. I need to pray."

"Just look at them," Jacek said to Berkovitz, who lay propped up by his elbow upon the heap of blankets next to him. He pointed to Moshe and Elias. "It seems as if they no longer hate each other."

"Well," Berkovitz said with a sigh, "so it would seem."

"When they first arrived at the barracks, they detested each other, and now . . ."

"Having death at hand can have a strange effect. Some become cowards, others become heroes."

"I never really believed that I was ever going to die."

"Everyone feels that way. Until they force you to file in, one after the other, into the incinerators."

"But even you had to have believed that you were invincible."

"Money certainly gives you that impression."

"Is it true, what you said earlier?"

"About the gold? With the help of a few friends, I managed to ship a large sum of it to Switzerland. And I saw to it that other reserves of mine were hidden away elsewhere, in a very secure location. But I'm not sure that I'll be able to use it here at camp. It's a lot like having a pistol locked in a case without a key—what good is it?"

Jacek propped himself up on his elbow and turned to Berkovitz.

"Money always finds its way into the hands of those who seek it. I am personal friends with many of the officers here. I could even go as far as Breitner."

"What do you have in mind?"

"Tell me where the money is hidden. The commander is unrelentingly greedy. He's stolen more from Kanada than everyone else put together."

"And I should trust you, I take it?"

"It's our only hope: we can buy a stay of execution from Breitner."

"He'll never let us out of here."

"No, perhaps you're right. But he might be willing to transfer us to the Ka-Be, as medical secretaries, or to the registrar even. We'd be in an office; warm, safe, and well fed. After that, we'd just need to wait until the end of the war."

"The end of the war . . . do you really believe that? You think that when the Russians arrive, the jackboots will just abandon their posts and hand us over as a cordial welcome offering? You're mad. Not one of us will leave here alive and we know why. Himmler will have each and every last prisoner exterminated, and he'll tell the world that we died in a typhus epidemic. They'll destroy the gas chambers, the crematoriums, the ramp; they'll say that nothing ever happened here. A POW camp, and nothing more. And they'll find someone who'll believe them. 'Millions of Jews murdered? Prove it!' "

"Think about it, Berkovitz, even if we make it through the night, we won't survive another winter here. The new detainees from Hungary will arrive; the selections will begin again. And you, with your glasses, assuredly won't pass."

Berkovitz's expression clouded over.

"No, I won't pass."

"And so, what do you have to lose? At least, this way, your gold will have served a purpose."

Berkovitz shook his head. "It's too late for me. My money won't carry me from this place. But I know it can prevent others from ending up here."

"I don't understand."

"Did you hear what Elias said earlier? They are preparing for mass deportations of prisoners from Hungary into the camps, just as they had done to us in Poland."

"Not even you have the buying power to save a million Jews."

"But I could persuade someone to intervene."

Jacek huffed.

"You're becoming an idle dreamer, much like he is"—he pointed to Otto—"or the others as well." He nodded in the direction of Paul and Elias. "You and I are very much the same, because you and I are the only ones who understand what it means to be impoverished."

"And how do you know that?"

"No one else here harbors the same anger as you or me, because they've never known real misery. But there lies our strength: we rely on and think only of ourselves. It is our only means of surviving within these walls."

"I used to believe that . . . before tonight. And yet, look at me, I ended up here in this nightmare. Both my wife and my daughter have taken refuge in Lausanne; luckily, at least I was wise enough to save them. And tonight, I learned that if you strive only to save yourself, you're going to end up at the bottom with everyone else."

Jacek leaned back upon the mound of blankets. He felt dizzy from his weakened state. When the barrack took to spinning round him, he shut his eyes. After having removed his glasses and placing them on the floor, Berkovitz closed his eyes, too.

"Look at that," Jiri whispered to Myriam. Her arms were wrapped around him, as if he were her child. Jiri was curled up tightly in a fetal position. "Jacek and Berkovitz, who knows what they're scheming. Those two frighten me."

With her eyes still closed, Myriam only shrugged.

"You haven't a thing to worry about; believe me, they are more frightened than we are."

They sat in silence, leaning against each other, listening to the sounds of their own hearts beating.

"Myriam?"

"Yes?"

"What's it like, having a child of your own?"

With eyes half closed she turned toward Jiri.

"I've always dreamed of having a child, you know. I'd like to know how it feels. To bring a human being into the world, who, without you, would never have existed. It's a little like playing God, don't you think?"

Myriam smiled. It was the first time that she had smiled since Ida had disappeared.

"I've never thought of it that way."

"I've always enjoyed the company of men. Even when I was little. In the showers, I'd always look at the other boys. I don't know why . . . my family was ordinary. But when my father found out, he locked me in the attic with the boy who lived downstairs; he beat me until I was black and blue. And I didn't hate it. I knew why he did it: he liked me. I think it was just his way of showing it."

Myriam squeezed him tighter.

"Having a child is . . . a strange feeling. When Ida was born and I held her for the first time, it was . . . strange. I thought that there must have been a mistake, that she could not have come from *me*. I'll tell you something that I've never told anyone, not even Elias. I *learned* to love Ida. There are women, and perhaps men, in this world, who are born to be parents. It's only natural for them to have someone to look after. All of a sudden, you come to realize that there is someone in the world who is more impor- tant than you. I had to learn that little by little. And then . . . and then she became my whole life. I learned to love her, and I've never stopped."

Myriam closed her eyes; her whole body shuddered, over- come with emotion.

"Maybe she's still alive," Jiri said reassuringly. "She was

blond, wasn't she? I've heard that often the SS kidnap children who can pass as Aryan and send them to German families."

Myriam smiled again. She passed her hand over his head, through the hair that had just started to grow again.

"I have a few friends in the SS," Jiri insisted, "They're the ones who told me about it. I'll bet that Ida is on a farm in Bavaria at this very moment. And after all, maybe there's some good to come of this. When the war is over you'll find her—"

But Myriam placed her hand to his mouth.

"There's no need," she said. "I know that Ida is no longer alive. And it isn't important whether there is someone to blame: myself, Elias, Hitler. Elias is right: it was God's will and there is nothing left for us to do."

"But you can survive! When the war is over—"

She stopped him again.

"Then what? When the war is over I could have another child, is that it? There could be nothing more horrible. It would be as if Ida were being *replaced* by another. Ida wasn't just a child; Ida was *my* child. There is not anything nor anyone that could replace her. Ever. I don't want to have any more children. Ever again."

"You always have Moshe."

Myriam smiled.

"He is a good man. He understood and consoled me. Elias prays and studies the Torah every hour of the day, hoping to find some justification for all that's happened. And even if he continues to declare that it was God's will, I know that he doesn't believe it himself. He cannot forgive himself for what he's done. And I . . . I hated him! I wanted to kill him! And had it not been for Moshe, perhaps I would have."

"But you—"

"I shouldn't have. I know. Elias was my husband. But there is no betrayal greater than his own. I stopped feeling as if I were married to him."

For a moment, Jiri was quiet.

He looked up to Myriam again. "Do you think that I could ever have a child of my own?"

"Of course. You just need to find the right woman."

"Yes, but . . . would they let me keep it?"

"The world will never be as we once knew it. So many things are changing out there. The war will cast away everything, and after, the world will be a better place. No longer will there be black, pink, or red triangles. Nor will there be Jews, Aryans, or blacks. We'll be fused into a great Babel of chaos, but this time, we won't set our sights on constructing a tower higher than the sky itself. Instead, we'll simply seek to live in peace with one another. Yes, Jiri, I am sure that, one day, you'll have a child of your own that you will be free to nurture and raise."

They held each other with the same tenderness as a mother and child.

Jiri softly sang a lullaby, one he could still recall from his childhood.

"*Z popielnika na Wojtusia . . . iskiereczka mruga . . .*"

Jiri felt Myriam's body slacken and relax.

"*Chodź opowiem ci bajeczke . . . Bajka będzie długa . . .*"

Every muscle in her body yielded to fatigue. Jiri sang his lullaby ever more softly while Myriam's breath took on a slow and steadied pace. She had drifted off to sleep.

And in that moment, the door to the barrack flung open. Oberscharführer Schmidt entered.

"Your soup is here," he announced with a stentorian tone.

0200 Hours

Alone in his study, Breitner was too restless to sleep. He had the feeling that he had left something undone, but he could not quite put his finger on it.

His eyes fell upon the chessboard. The black pieces were scattered about the board without any apparent strategy. Felix would never be much of a player. Nevertheless, his passion might carry him. The commandant moved to the opposite end of the board and studied the situation. In his mind, chess was much like plotting the convergence of opposing forces: both sides seeking protection for their pieces, escape routes, and a means of attack.

All of the sudden, he sighed, struck by a sudden revelation. Heeding his intuition, he leaned to each side of the board, eyeing the pieces with great care. Yes, perhaps it could be done. . . .

Breitner then moved the white knight. Without stopping to consider his play, he promptly repositioned the black bishop. One move after the other, the pieces slid across the chessboard, obeying the rigid geometry of the game. Breitner was now hopelessly immersed. He relinquished a pawn and a rook, and then stopped for a moment to study the result of his line of attack. He tried to keep both forces an equal stance apart. On one side, he had drawn

a strategy of his own, and on the opposite end, he sought to follow the tactics that an amateur might seek. *Yes,* he resolved after
a moment's reflection; there were considerable risks, but it was
feasible. Taking great care, he took hold of the knight and held it
up with his middle and index finger. From beyond the window,
the camp, the towers, the guards, the searchlights, the crematorium, and the gas chambers had all but disappeared. All that mattered was his game of chess.

"Goddamnit!" the Oberscharführer clamored as he entered the
washhouse. "What the hell is the commander thinking, serving
Wassersuppe at this hour. Christ! What are we, a five-star resort?"

He held the door open, allowing two *Häftlinge* to enter the
barrack; numb from the cold and enfeebled by their fatigue, they
shuffled in, each lugging one end of a large stick over their shoulder. From it hung a piping hot *Kübel* that measured a hundred
litres in volume. At camp, there were no pots of smaller propor-
tions.

"We've had to open the kitchen for our esteemed guests,"
grumbled the now aggravated warrant officer.

The two *Häftlinge* let the vat drop to the ground with a thud,
and promptly rubbed their hands against the sleeves of their uniforms in an effort to fight the cold. They exited the washhouse,
and, after a moment, returned carrying eight mess tins.

"*Los!*" roared the Oberscharführer. "Get your mess tins and
come here at once!"

Jacek bolted upright. Sitting up, he placed his hands on the
ground; pain thrashed through his veins, his blood struggled to
circulate. He grabbed Berkovitz by the arm and shook him from
his sleep.

"Berkovitz, Berkovitz, come on. There's soup."

Startled, the financier's eyes flung open. For a brief moment, he could not recall where he was, but he quickly regained his sense of reality. His hands groped the floor in search of his glasses, which he then swiftly slid upon the bridge of his nose.

"All right, I'm coming."

Jiri woke Myriam.

"Myriam, Myriam, the soup is here."

"Mmm . . ." She was limp with sleep. "I don't want any. You go ahead."

"You need to eat, Myriam. You can't stay like this. Come on, I'll help you."

Though he struggled, he managed to cross her arms behind her back, then, with a shove, he pushed her upright. Her head fell limply backward.

"Come on, Myriam, get up!"

The *Häftlinge*'s deficient speeds only fueled the Oberscharführer's anger.

"Pieces of shit! *Los!*"

Moshe, who had been seated upon the floor, shifted to his feet.

He offered his hand to Elias, which the rabbi grasped, but despite his hold, he was unable to pull himself to his feet.

"I can't, Moshe. I'm too tired."

"You have to, Elias. Come on, try."

Otto and Paul rose from their places at the table.

"All right, who's first?" the Oberscharführer asked.

The prisoners exchanged furtive glances. No one wanted to be first. They knew that the first servings consisted of mostly liquid, while the potatoes and turnips—if there were any to be had—would be at the bottom of the pot.

"Okay, let's go, here I am."

Moshe held out his mess tin; one of the two *Häftlinge* who had arrived with the soup served him. He eyed Moshe with hostility:

evidently he blamed him for the unpleasant late-night rouse. The prisoner dipped the ladle into the steaming broth and clumsily poured just over half a liter into Moshe's tin.

"Next."

"Let's go! Over here!" Otto handed over his bowl.

The prisoner haphazardly emptied three or four spoonfuls into his tray, some of which splattered onto Otto's uniform.

"Watch out!"

"Next."

It was Myriam's turn. The presence of a woman frightened the prisoner; he hastily poured her a hefty serving of soup.

"Hey, Samuel, you trying to impress the lady?" the SS officer asked. "That's enough. Hurry up, we all want to go back to bed!"

They served Jiri, who displayed his gratitude with a ceremonial bow; he knew that whatever he did mattered very little, for that night they would remain untouchable. Then came Paul, Berkovitz, and Jacek. In the barrack leader's bowl floated a solitary potato.

"Lucky catch, eh, Jacek?" Moshe said.

Only Elias remained; he was still seated on the floor.

Moshe placed his tin on the table, and carted him to his feet. But Moshe was very weak, too. Paul came to their aid. The German had little difficulty lifting the rabbi's meager frame.

"Hurry up, you damned Jew!" roared the Oberscharführer, whose patience had evaporated. "The commander ordered that you receive soup, and I will obey accordingly! But, if you don't hurry up—"

Elias was on his feet. He teetered, fighting to overcome his weakness. Moshe handed him his tin and nudged him forcefully toward the pot. The prisoner in charge of divvying out the portions held out a spoonful, waiting impatiently to be relinquished of his duties.

"*Schnell!*" shouted the now enraged SS officer.

The prisoner, who had grown accustomed to the mess rations, hurriedly slopped three or four spoonfuls into Elias's tin; for he knew and feared the wrath of the warrant officer.

Elias's bowl was now full. The rabbi turned to go.

"Wait," the warrant officer ordered, "that isn't a sufficient amount."

The Oberscharführer snatched the ladle away from the prisoner. He then plunged it into the *Wassersuppe*; lifting it from the pot, he glanced to ensure that the spoon was full. He then held it toward Elias. The officer's face bore a pernicious sneer.

"Here you are, Jew."

Extending his arm to where Elias now stood, the officer suddenly threw the boiling soup at him.

The rabbi, shocked, staggered backward, groaning with pain.

"Oh, how careless of me," the Oberscharführer observed with a querulous tone. "I don't know what I was thinking."

Elias fell to the floor. The soup saturated his uniform from his chest to his knees. His mess tin had spilled over, and the soup had now formed into a vast puddle on the floor. Moshe leaned down to help him.

"You. Stop. Don't move," the officer warned.

With a rigid military gait, the SS approached the defenseless man, looming over him from above.

"Rabbi! Your uniform is now breaching regulation. Have you no shame? Look at how filthy you are!"

Confounded by the events, Elias struggled to follow the words of the SS officer.

"You must change! Immediately!"

Elias looked up at the Oberscharführer; his face was shrouded by a despondent expression, one that the warrant officer ignored.

"Get up, you Jewish pig. Get up!"

Employing the little energy he had left, Elias managed to sit on his knees on the floor. Then, gathering his strength, he propped his arm upon his thigh and pulled himself to his feet. His sodden uniform clung to his body, emanating the smell of hot food.

The Oberscharführer's pupils glared directly into those of Elias. The officer was now but a few inches from the prisoner.

"Did you not hear? I said, undress! You are in violation of the rules, you are not permitted to stay as such!"

Elias looked on with a stolid gaze.

"Is there soup in your ear? Undress immediately!"

The Oberscharführer seized the club that had been fastened to his belt and held it menacingly over the prisoner's head.

The rabbi, quivering, began to undo the top button of his jacket.

"*Schnell!*" the officer roared in his face.

His coat, saturated with soup, hugged tightly to his emaciated torso. After a moment, it fell to the floor. Beneath it, his shirt was soiled, too.

"Pants! *Schnell!*" the SS spurred him on.

Elias let his trousers fall to the floor. Bandages covered both his stomach and bony thighs.

"Hurry up!" the guard warned once again.

Elias placed his trousers atop the stinking pile of his jacket. The Oberscharführer looked on with a contented stare as he tapped his club into the palm of his hand.

"Good! And now see to it that you find a clean uniform. It shouldn't be difficult given that you're in the washhouse—"

He stopped short. Something had caught his eye. His hand reached toward Elias. The rabbi stood, immobile.

"What is this?"

The SS pointed to the corner edge of paper that, ever so slightly, protruded from the upper folds of the soiled bandage wrapped across his stomach. Elias lowered his eyes and kept his expression neutral.

The Oberscharführer grabbed the corner of the paper and pulled it out, eyeing it with a triumphant smile.

"A photograph!"

Elias stared at the precious object in disbelief; it was the one thing that, up until that very moment, had given him the will to survive.

"And who might this be?" the SS asked. "Your little whore?"

Elias shook. His fists clenched. Moshe eyed Elias, as if to urge him to keep his composure. But there was no need. The rabbi made not a sound, though his eyes seethed with rage.

"You do know that the regulations categorically prohibit the possession of any personal property? I'll have to punish you."

The SS snickered. He had found his revenge for the extra work he had had to do. In one hand he held the photograph just out of Elias's reach, and in the other, he held his club, which he tapped rhythmically against his leg.

"The photo has been appropriated," he announced, waving the object just shy of Elias's face.

"Please, Oberscharführer, I beg you," Elias murmured.

"What's that? You dare address a warrant officer without permission?"

"Herr Oberscharführer, I beg you . . . it is the only photograph that I have of my daughter. She disappeared a few months ago. . . . It is the only thing I have left of her."

The SS listened with an insolent grin. His club swung up and down, up and down, and each time it met the officer's leg, a menacing sound echoed through the barrack.

"Please . . ."

A tear trickled down the rabbi's gaunt cheek.

"I beg you."

"Herr Oberscharführer!" It was Berkovitz. The SS, bewildered, spun on his heel.

"Herr Oberscharführer," Berkovitz began as he took a step toward the officer, "Elias is not well; he has not eaten since early this morning and he is terribly weak. If you'd be so kind as to give him—"

"You're all insane, every one of you!" The SS officer's sneer had abruptly transformed into an expression that teemed with rage. "The fact that the commander is protecting you doesn't give you the right to utter even a word to me. Is that understood?"

For a moment, Berkovitz lingered, uncertain as to how to respond. He opened his mouth as if to say something, and then, thinking better of it, turned and retreated from the scene.

"Come on, Johann," Moshe said coaxingly in his customary casual tone. "There's no need for you to look so grim. Anyway, you know why we're here."

The SS turned toward Moshe.

"I don't know anything about it; I'm just following orders."

"Come on . . . for one of us here, tonight is going to be the last. Look the other way for once, won't you?" And with a magician's grace, his pulled two cigarettes from beneath his jacket. He handed them to the officer. The Oberscharführer tucked his club under his arm and took the cigarettes. His eyed Moshe with an air of approval.

"Ibars . . . very nice. How did you manage to come across these?"

"I placed an order for them from the store down on the corner. They're open all night." Moshe grinned.

From the same mysterious hidden pocket, he extracted a lighter with an intricately tooled handle.

"Here you are."

The SS slipped his club back into place on his belt. He placed one cigarette in his pocket and the other in his mouth. He grabbed hold of the lighter and sparked the flame.

"Very nice," he said with admiration. "Well, Moshe, even if you are damned . . . you certainly know how to get by in this world, don't you?"

The guard eyed the flame. He raised the lighter to the far end of his cigarette. In his other hand, he still held the photograph. Elias's eyes remained fixed upon his lone heirloom. Officer Schmidt savored the flavor of three or four drags from his cigarette. He kept the lighter in his hand, showing no signs of returning it.

"Magnificent." He exhaled. Then, promptly resuming his military airs, he addressed the prisoners.

"Go ahead and continue your little meeting. Notify me when you have made a decision. You have until 0600."

He turned on his heels.

"Johann," Moshe called out.

The Oberscharführer turned only his head.

"Yes, Moshe? You had something to say?"

"The photo," Moshe said with a nod of his chin.

"The commander ordered that I report all findings to him. The photo has been sequestered."

Upon hearing those words, Elias fell into a state of desperation.

"Ida!" the rabbi cried; he flung himself forward in an effort to seize the picture. Yet the warrant officer sensed—or perhaps had predicted his reaction—and with ease, he moved aside, circumventing the attack. Elias, blinded by his rage, missed his target. The SS let the lighter fall to the floor and then grabbed hold of his club. He swung it over his head and delivered a violent blow to the rabbi's shoulders.

Elias had opportunity to take cover and cried out in pain as

he tumbled to the floor. The Oberscharführer stood over him
and dealt him a series of blows, first to his back and then to his
sides. Every agonizing grunt only helped to incite the officer's
rage. His club laid into Elias's skull.

"*Arschloch!* How dare you assault a German! I'll teach you a
lesson!"

The thrashing was accompanied only by the sound of flaccid,
beaten flesh. Blood trickled from Elias's ear across the floor. The
rabbi was immobile. His body had been reduced to a crushed
bundle of flesh. None of the other seven had the courage to intervene. They watched the atrocity in silence. Even the two *Häftlinge*
who had brought the soup watched, petrified by the sight.

"Enough, Johann, that's enough," Moshe mustered the courage to mutter.

And then, just as quickly as it had erupted, his rage subsided.
The Oberscharführer stopped. He was panting heavily and
drenched with sweat. He readjusted his uniform across his front
and distanced himself by a step. When he saw that his club was
soiled with blood, he knelt down and wiped it clean using one
end of Elias's shirttail that had been abandoned on the floor.

The SS stared at the rabbi's body.

"I'll have to report this to the commander," he said, almost
inaudibly. "He won't be happy."

He exited, alongside the two *Häftlinge*, slamming the door
behind them.

"Come on, give me a hand," Moshe said. "Let's lay him on a
blanket."

With the greatest care, Moshe, Berkovitz, Jiri, and Paul lifted
Elias. The rabbi's head had been split open and part of his face
had been left black and blue, but he was still breathing.

"Be careful!" Moshe cautioned as they placed him on a mound
of blankets situated in one of the darker corners of the room.

Myriam kneeled on the floor next to her husband. She stroked his chest, and then turned toward the others, her eyes burning.

"Go away!"

"Myriam," Moshe said.

"Leave!" she screamed. She leaned over her husband and wrapped her arms around him, his blood soaking her uniform.

"Elias."

The rabbi gave no answer.

The commandant, who was still in his study and wholly immersed in the game, heard a knock at the door. He peered up at the grandfather clock, an ornate piece embossed in gold; it had, much like all of the rest of the furniture, been brought from Kanada. Some Jew had been foolish enough to drag it with him on the train. He heard the knock again, leaving Breitner rather vexed. *Who the hell . . . ?* A feverish angst had taken hold of him, as if the outcome of his game was of great importance.

Irritated, he got up and threw open the door. There, in front of him, stood the Oberscharführer.

"Herr Schmidt! You've come! They've come to a decision then!"

"No, Herr Kommandant!"

"Has there been an incident?"

"A prisoner attempted to assault me. I was forced to defend myself."

"Is he dead?"

"I don't believe so. But he is badly wounded. Should I have him transferred to the Ka-Be?"

"No. Leave him. His inmates will see to it that he is looked after. Who was it? The rabbi, by chance?"

The lieutenant could not mask his amazement.

"Exactly, Herr Kommandant. That's precisely who it was."

"Just another pawn," Breitner's voice tapered off with a sigh.

"What's that, Herr Offizier?"

"Nothing. What happened, exactly?"

"The prisoner attempted to conceal a photograph beneath his uniform."

All at once, the commandant's eyes lit up with interest.

"A photograph? Of what?"

"A photo of a little girl. Here it is."

The warrant officer removed the photograph from his pocket and handed it to his superior. Breitner took the photograph without much apparent interest, but when he caught sight of the image, his face grew ashen.

"It was this photograph? Are you sure?"

"He had it hidden in his clothing," repeated the warrant officer.

He had never before seen the commandant lose his composure.

Breitner continued to stare at the photograph; he seemed to have forgotten everything else around him. A few minutes passed and the lieutenant waited at attention; he then cleared his throat in order to call the attention of the commandant.

"Yes?" Breitner asked, barely raising his eyes.

"Herr Kommandant, are there any other orders?"

"No, Herr Oberscharführer. That will be all. If anything else should occur, you are to alert me immediately."

The warrant officer stalked off, his heels sounding with each step.

Breitner returned to his desk. He sat down and opened a box. From among the many files, he removed a dossier that had been tucked into a brown folder.

He leafed through the reports, which had been typed, complete with second copies, though the letter O had punctured the carbon paper. He sifted slowly through the pages until he found what he was looking for.

A photograph.

A little girl.

Breitner grabbed the photo that had been delivered by the lieutenant, and placed it next to the other. He stared at them for a long while, studying every detail.

The blond hair, the braids, the blue eyes, the smile.

There was no doubt. It was the same girl.

The commander couldn't help but grin.

Breitner, feeling rather amused, placed the photograph he received from the officer into the folder, and filed it away in the box. Fate never ceased to amaze him.

He pondered the extraordinary chain of events, and returned once again to the chessboard.

0300 Hours

"All right, what do we want to do?"

Jacek, feeling revived after a bowl of hot soup, nervously paced back and forth in the area of the barrack where light from the bulb still shone.

"There's not much time left for us. We need to decide."

The others—Jiri, Moshe, Berkovitz, Paul, and Otto—avoided his gaze. Myriam was on the other side of the clothesline, tending to her dying husband.

"All right then, what do you say? Otto, what do you think?"

The politician turned his head the other way. Jacek approached him.

"Otto!" He seized him by the arm, forcing him to turn around. "Otto! Was it not you, who, only a few hours ago, wanted all of this to end as quickly as possible? Weren't you the one in a rush to carry out your much anticipated escape?"

Otto shook his head.

"Let me be."

Otto yanked his arm in attempts to free himself, but Jacek would not release his grip.

"Don't you get it? If we don't decide something soon, the

commander is going to kill us all. Then, you won't have the possibility of escaping, and your comrades' little operation will be useless."

"I said, let me be!"

But Jacek was overcome with frenzied thought.

"We still have the chance to decide. Elias is over there, half dead. He is most likely not going to make it. We have to hurry before—"

But before Jacek could finish, Otto spun around and slapped him with such force that the Kapo fell to the ground.

"Shut up!"

Jacek, with his back still to the floor, slid backward to a safe distance. He cupped the cheek that Alexey had battered with the palm of his hand.

"You're all mad," he wheezed as he slinked farther away. "We risk having every one of us executed."

On the other side of the clothesline, Myriam tended to her husband as best she could. Elias was lying on the floor. Blood had saturated the blankets, and his face was distorted from the blows that had smashed the right side of his skull. One eye had been dislodged from its socket, attached only by way of its optical nerve. The rabbi groaned in agony. His labored breathing emitted a terrible sound; his lungs, having not wanted to give way, continued forcing air into what seemed to be a body on the verge of death. Myriam wiped his brow with a piece of damp cloth.

Otto crossed the room and passing the uniforms hanging on the clothesline, he made his way toward Myriam and Elias.

"What do you want?" she asked without turning her head.

"I studied medicine," Otto said, "I can help him."

He took a seat next to Myriam, and placed his fingers on the side of Elias's neck.

"His pulse is very weak."

The rabbi's eyes were clouded; Elias weakly cried out in pain as his body trembled in sporadic fits.

"He's suffering a great deal," Myriam contested despondently.

"Hold on. I have something for him." From within the folds of his uniform, Otto extracted a small, crude cloth bag. He opened it and removed a minuscule hypodermic needle. Jacek and Moshe appeared, watching over the German's shoulders.

"What is that?" Myriam asked.

"Morphine. We were able to procure some while at the *Revier*, a precautionary measure for the escape, in the event that something went wrong."

"How did you manage to get that?" Jacek's eyes burned feverishly.

"Not even the soldiers on the front line have it!"

"I told you, We took it from the *Revier*."

"Do you see that!" Jacek shouted as he turned in the direction of the others. "He has morphine! He's a spy! There's your proof! They gave it to him in case anything happened in here with us!"

"Let it go, Jacek," Moshe warned. The barrack leader quieted, though his face was still flushed with both rage and fear.

Otto grabbed the syringe and injected the needle into Elias's arm. After a few minutes, the rabbi's tremors had ceased and his breathing seemed to have regained a steady pace.

The politician checked the rabbi's pulse once more.

"He's not in any pain; at least, I don't think he is."

"But, now, what will you do? Your escape?" Myriam said, with a look filled with gratitude.

Otto only shrugged. "It wasn't essential. I was never able to help my father or my brother; at least I can do something for Elias. As for the escape . . . it's useless now."

"That isn't true," Moshe interjected, "There's still time."

Otto huffed with skepticism. "How exactly? We've been locked in here since yesterday afternoon. In a few hours, when the *Arbeitskommandos* leave, my comrades will be on the move, with or without me. In a short while, dawn will have arrived, and I will still be locked in here. I won't make it."

Jacek interrupted, addressing the others. "Did you hear that? He's a spy! That's proof right there! First, he tells us of his plans to escape, then he says it's no longer possible. It's just his ploy to see if we bite!"

"Enough of that, Jacek," Jiri said. "We've already heard it before, try the next page of your script; give us some new material."

"The operation was never a work of fiction," Otto objected harshly. "And I can prove it." Turning to Jacek, he asked, "You'll keep quiet about this, won't you? If not, my comrades will hang you by your own entrails. And you, Paul?"

The German flashed a sardonic grin. "What's that? You don't trust me?"

"Think of it as a family reunion," Moshe said. "Growing up in your castle in Bavaria, I'm sure you were put to bed when the grown-ups had matters to discuss."

"That's fine, whatever you want. I'll be there in the back. Call me once you're finished with your little secrets."

He made his way past the others, glancing toward Myriam and then Elias, who still lay unconscious on the floor. He then disappeared past the clothesline and into the dark corner of the barrack.

Otto waited, saying not a word until Paul was out of earshot. The others converged around the table, while the bleak light of the bulb cast spectral shadows upon their faces from above.

He then began, in a voice no louder than a whisper. "As you might know, a few weeks ago, the jackboots started construction on a new unit, just outside of the recesses of the camp. They call it Mexico. The *Arbeitskommandos* have already unloaded a considerable amount of wood brought in by train."

"It's true," Jiri confirmed, "there are stacks of it."

"And that is where we intend to hide out."

"In the wood piles?"

"We were able to infiltrate the *Arbeitskommandos* where they are working. During the day, it isn't difficult to disappear among the hundreds of *Häftlinge* who are working there. When you go to the toilet or go for a serving of *Wassersuppe*. Myself and two others will be there hidden away underneath."

"The alarms will sound for three days, you know that."

"And we will remain there for three days."

"They'll find you. They have dogs."

"We thought of that, too. Tobacco soaked in petroleum: the magic formula. Even the most skilled hound can't track you if you douse yourself with petroleum and tobacco."

"And after the three days?"

"You know as well as I. The external alarms at each watchtower are deactivated and everything goes back to normal. The camp authorities are no longer obligated to search for the escapees. We will be outside of the walls and en route to our Polish comrades within the AK."

Silence hung about the barrack. Each one of them—apart from Myriam and Elias, who remained in the dark corner of the barrack—contemplated Otto's words.

"It's a trap, don't you see?" Jacek erupted. "He wants you to—"

"Enough!" Moshe interjected. He turned to the others, glancing at each, one by one. And though his height had not changed, he suddenly seemed to be eyeing the others from above. "I believe him."

"Really, Moshe," Berkovitz objected, "you were the one who trusted him the least; just a few hours ago you were convinced he was a spy."

Moshe answered with only a shrug. "You're right. Only a few hours ago I thought he was a spy planted here by the commander. But I've changed my mind. I don't know why exactly. Perhaps because of what he's told us, or perhaps it was the morphine. Whatever the reason, I know he's told us the truth."

"And even if it was," Berkovitz countered. "What ties do you have to the party? It is of no importance to you."

"I'm not concerned in the slightest with the party. But we'd show the jackboots that, even under their seamless command, we could still pull one over on them. If anything, I'd die happy knowing that. Otto needs our help."

"Help him!" Jiri said. "How the hell are we going to help him?"

"I don't know. But at the least, we'll have to try. The commander—"

"The commander will kill every one of us if we don't provide him a name in three hours' time," Jacek said.

"The commander is going to kill us all regardless," Moshe continued, taking no notice of Jacek. "Have you forgotten what they tell the prisoners as they arrive? A shower to disinfect, and then you'll have milk, butter, bread . . . a shower. . . . The SS always lie. Breitner is thoroughly enjoying all of this, but when he tires of it, you better believe that he'll send every one of us to the *Krematorium*. And so, yes, we must help Otto escape."

"But if—" Jacek began, still with the intention to voice his objections.

"'In fleeing death, men seek it,'" Jiri recited. "It's a relief that we're all dead men."

"True," Berkovitz, who had been quiet until that moment, suddenly concurred. "Jiri is right. We're all dead men. Be it at dawn, or shortly after, or even a month from now, we won't escape our fate. But that's precisely what makes us that much stronger. No one can touch us."

"Listen," Moshe began, "I now know why the commander chose to lock us up in here."

"To kill us, right?" Jacek said.

"Yes, but not only that. We are like the tiles of a mosaic. We are each but an insignificant, minute tile, in a design that is much greater than all of us here. For this reason, at first anyway, I felt as if there was nothing we could do. But then"—his tone grew serious—"but then, when the guard struck Elias, it came to me. Yes, we are just insignificant fragments of a grand design that is much greater than any of us, but if we unite, if we join together in perfect accord, each one linked with the other, then a small portion of that whole will begin to make sense. Alone, we account for nothing. Do you know why we all ended up here? Because each of us has always thought only of ourselves. You, Berkovitz, thought only of money. Elias, poor thing, thought only of his religion. Jiri, his theater and his men. And I, too, thought only of my business affairs. Even Myriam . . . she, though better than the rest of us, thought only of her family. We were blind to what was happening around us. We deemed politics a dirty endeavor, one in which we consented never to meddle. But there comes a moment when you are forced to partake."

Berkovitz gathered the pieces of paper they had used in their first vote, then lifting his hand to the side of his face, he let the pieces fall. The scraps floated slowly toward the floor. From beneath his scratched lenses, his eyes burned brightly.

"Pieces of a mosaic . . ."

"If we join forces," Moshe continued, "the end result will be much greater than the sum of any of our own efforts. It is only in this way that we can achieve something. Perhaps it will be but a small feat. Or perhaps it will be something of great consequence."

Silence fell upon the *Wäscherei*. Even Myriam listened from a distance.

"He's right," Berkovitz concluded. "Moshe is right."

"Now you, Berkovitz!" Jacek's voice broke into a screech. "You, who has always thought only of your money!"

"I am accustomed to facing reality, even if it is harsh. I can detect when a company is headed toward ruin and there is nothing that can be done. I am much too old to survive the KZ. But before I leave here, there is still good that I can do. I'm with you, Moshe; I'll do everything I can to help."

With that, the financier stretched open his mouth and pointed inside it. "Here, in one of my lower molars, there is a diamond hidden. The SS and the medics could never detect it because it was encased inside a perfect porcelain crown. I had it done by the best dentist in all of London. In truth, I never harbored much faith in Hitler. It won't do me any good in here. If anyone found out, I'd be killed for having it. But outside, the diamond can easily be sold, and that money will be useful to you during the escape. It's only right that you take it, Otto."

"I . . ." vacillated the politician.

"Take it. At least it will have been of some use. Rather than ending up as a ring to show off at a soirée, this diamond will help save the lives of others. Now, we only need to pull it out."

"What did the dentist say?"

"That it wouldn't be difficult. A quick tug of a lever, or something of that sort."

"It's going to hurt."

"Not much. At least he assured me it wouldn't. And, at any rate, it doesn't matter. Let's do this, quickly."

Otto looked around, in search of something they could use.

"The knife," suggested Moshe.

"Ah, yes. Alexey's knife. Where did it go?"

They found it lodged beneath a heap of blankets, where it had slid during the fight. Otto grabbed hold of it.

"It would be best to disinfect it."

"How exactly?" Moshe asked.

"All you need is fire. Get your lighter."

Moshe retrieved the lighter that the SS had pitched to the ground.

They held the blade just above the flame, on one side and then the other until the metal turned bronze.

Berkovitz took a seat, his legs spread. He draped his arms around the back of the chair.

"Someone hold me down."

Moshe stood at his shoulders, wrapping his arm just beneath his lower jaw. Jiri held him by the wrists, preventing any movement.

"I'm ready," Berkovitz announced.

The Red moved closer and leaned down to better peer into Berkovitz's mouth.

"Which is it?"

"The second molar. On the left. Do it quickly."

Otto carefully inserted the blade of the knife into Berkovitz's mouth, placing it on his gums.

"This one?"

"Mmm-hmm," the financier answered with a whimper.

Moshe held open Berkovitz's mouth

"It will only take a second," Otto reassured him. He rotated his wrist to better steady himself against his patient's jawbone, and then pushed with all his might. Sweat started to gather on his forehead.

"Mmm-hmm," Berkovitz groaned in pain.

"One second . . . just one second. . . ."

One last tug. The tooth gave way as the blade slipped to one side. Otto managed to steady the knife so that the blade narrowly missed lodging itself in Berkovitz's palate. The financier bent forward, spurting blood. They stared at the floor. There, in the middle of a bloody puddle, a diamond glistened, still encased in porcelain.

"Here it is," Berkovitz said. He picked up the rock with two fingers, wiped it clean on his jacket, and then held it up for the others to see.

"Beautiful," Jiri said admiringly. With his thumb and forefinger, he took the diamond and held it suspended just under his earlobe, as if it were an earring. "Ladies, how do I look?"

"It cost a fortune. I never imagined that it would have ended up in this state," Berkovitz said after having spat more blood onto the floor.

"And now? How are we going to get out of here?" Otto implored.

"I have an idea," Moshe said. "We—"

Just then, Paul appeared from behind the hanging uniforms.

"Have you finished you family reunion?"

"Come on then."

The German approached guardedly.

"Well, look at these worried little faces. I get the impression that you discussed more than the usual ghetto gossip," he said as he circled the table, eyeing each of them.

"What were you all doing with Berkovitz?"

"Removing plaque," Moshe answered. "He had a great deal of it."

"You Jews can be quite crafty. Small but precious things can be hidden, say, in a tooth."

The others were silent.

"So is that it? Am I right?"

"What does it matter? In here, you're no different than the rest of us."

Paul paid no attention.

"Perhaps you were struck by an idea. Tonight's course of events has certainly changed you. You are no longer the same feeble, ridiculous Jews who trembled in the face of the slightest threat."

"No," Moshe said, "We're no longer that type of Jew." He rose to his feet.

"You know what I think? That you're planning to escape. Some trivial, pathetic attempt to flee. It's your beau geste, am I right? You know very well that you'll never get out of here alive."

"Yes, so we've been told," Moshe answered as moved closer to Paul.

"And just how do you intend to do it?" Paul asked. "How do you plan on making it past the electric fence, the watchtowers, the guards, the dogs? It's impossible, don't you see that?"

As he spoke, he moved almost imperceptibly in the direction of the door. Moshe followed, staying a few feet back. They moved across the floor, each keeping a circumspect watch on the other. They moved with short quick steps, like dancers awaiting a cue from their partner to begin.

"Spot-on. You're precisely right, it's impossible," Moshe answered. "There's nothing to fear with this little cowardly group of Jews."

With that, Paul sprang toward the door. He managed to grab hold of the handle, but before he could open the door, Moshe attacked.

"Stop!" he bellowed.

The German buried an elbow in Moshe's stomach. Moshe fell

back, gasping. Before the German could open the door, Otto and
Berkovitz hurled themselves upon him. The two prisoners fought
to pin down both his arms and legs, while the officer thrashed
about like a madman, struggling to free himself from their hold.
Jiri stood with his back fastened to the wall, paralyzed with terror. With eyes splayed wide, he followed the struggle, unable to
muster the courage to move. Even Jacek stood immobile, observ-
ing the brawl with no intent to intervene.

"Oberscharführer!" Paul yelled as he fought off his attackers.
"Oberscharführer! The prisoners are trying to esca—"

"Shut up, Nazi!" Berkovitz snarled as shoved his hand into
Paul's mouth, to which the German countered by violently sinking his teeth into the financier's hand. Berkovitz hastily retracted
his hand and tumbled to the floor, clutching the wound. Otto
held fast to the officer's legs, but he managed to free himself, and
then he turned and pummeled Otto squarely in the face with his
fist. The politician lay on the floor, stunned by the blow.

The German picked up the knife from off the ground, the
same knife that had been used to extract the diamond, and made
for Otto's neck. With scarcely a second to spare, the politician
seized Paul's wrist, blocking the attack, but the officer's strength
overpowered him; millimeter after millimeter, the tip of the
knife neared Otto's jugular.

"Jiri!" Otto implored.

The Pink Triangle was frozen with fear, incapable of moving so much as a finger. Moshe was still on the ground, gasping
for air.

Berkovitz started to crawl to his feet in an effort to reach
Otto, but Paul, without deigning so much as a glance, abruptly
arched back and thrusting his leg rearward delivered a sharp blow
to Berkovitz's lower abdomen. The financier collapsed to the floor

with a whimper. Again the Nazi lurched forward, ready to impale the politician's throat. So close was the blade, it seemed Otto had little hope of escaping.

"Jiri," Otto pleaded, now hoarse from his struggle to fend off the Nazi.

With his face contorted by nervous tension, the Pink Triangle suddenly hurled himself toward the officer. It would be the first time in his life in which he found himself in the midst of a brawl; even as a child he had always been careful to avoid a scuffle with his peers. Without knowing precisely what to do, he seized Paul by the wrist in an effort to gain control of the blade. The officer's hold deviated and the knife veered off to the side. And though it was not Paul's intent, the blade sank into Jiri's side. Paul held steadily to the knife, and with a curt tug, he pulled the blade from the wound and rose to his feet. Otto scrambled away.

For an instant, Jiri stared at his side in astonishment, as if to make sure that he was the one that had been struck. Only when blood started to flow did Jiri begin to panic. He fell to his knees, clutching his wound. He cried and whimpered, just as a small child might have.

"Oh God . . . it *hurts.* Help me, please, help me . . ."

"Stupid Jews!" Paul hissed as he waved the blade for the others to see. "Did you really think that I'd let you escape? I may be a prisoner, but I am still a soldier of the Third Reich—"

His last words fell short. The sound of a sharp crack echoed through the barrack. Paul's eyes fluttered and then he crashed to the ground, unconscious.

Myriam stood behind him. She was breathing heavily; above her head she clutched a chair. One of its wooden legs had snapped off from the force of the impact.

"Myriam!" Moshe called out.

But the woman did not hear him. She held fast to the chair as if prepared to deliver another blow. Her eyes were wide with fury; she drew great heaving breaths.

Moshe knelt down next to Hauser. The officer was prostrate, stretched out across the floor. He groaned in pain. Straining to get to his feet, his arms and legs slowly passed over the floor. His eyes were still partially closed from the blow.

"He's still unconscious," Moshe said. "But he won't be for much longer. What do we do?"

Berkovitz looked on with a troubled air. Jiri cried out unremittingly, clutching his side with blood-soaked hands. Jacek remained stationary, having not moved since the start of the brawl.

Otto searched the floor. When he spotted what he was looking for, he knelt to the ground and picked it up. He turned toward the others. In his hand, he clutched Alexey's knife, still stained with Jiri's blood. His fingers slid across the handle's slick surface.

"Get out of the way," he told Moshe, at which the other promptly distanced himself.

Otto, wielding the knife, bent forward over the Nazi. With much effort, he managed to roll the listless body faceup. Only then did Jacek move, crossing toward the Red.

Otto looked up furiously.

"What's it to you, Jacek? Now you want to save your master?"

For a moment, each faced the other in silence, and then the Kapo made his retreat.

Otto gripped the handle of the blade, and without a hint of hesitation, he slit Hauser's throat. A gush of blood steeped his uniform. Hauser's eyes abruptly flung open as his body released a final quiver. His eyes bore a stunned, almost grievous look about them. His expression then dimmed; his eyes closed. The stream of blood weakened and began to slowly drip down upon the fur collar of his leather jacket. The SS's body contracted in his death throes until the life within him altogether ceased.

Moshe drew back, horrified. "Otto . . ."

The Red turned toward Moshe, still clutching the blood-stained knife. "What did you want to happen? You wanted to let him live so he could warn the others about us? Is it not your God who taught 'an eye for an eye, a tooth for a tooth'?"

Moshe tore his eyes away from the Nazi's corpse, around which a puddle of blood had formed. He then rushed to Jiri's aid, who still lay gasping on the floor. With his hands clutched tightly at his side, he wept like a child. He grabbed hold of Moshe's jacket, pulling him close, his hands drenched in blood.

"I'm going to die, aren't I? I'm dying, I know it. . . . *Aah,* it hurts so much. . . . Help me, please, I beg you, help me . . ." he sobbed.

"Let's move you over there, to where the blankets are."

Jiri nodded in consent, but when Moshe, along with Otto and Berokovitz, tried to lift him, he cried out in agony.

"Stop!" he pleaded. "Just leave me here."

They placed him gently on the floor. Myriam took a blanket, rolled it up, and slid it under his head as a cushion.

Otto knelt down next to him. "Let me have a look."

But Jiri clutched resolutely to his side.

"I said, let me look," Otto repeated brusquely.

"Swear to me that you won't hurt me . . . the pain is unbearable . . . *Aah* . . . help me . . ."

"How can I help you if you won't even let me have a look?"

Jiri gave in. He opened his arms and closed his eyes. He grimaced in pain.

Otto tore open Jiri's uniform, exposing the wound.

"Grab something from Paul's body, either his shirt or his pants."

Myriam assisted Moshe; as he lifted each leg, Myriam removed the pant's leg. Otto then tore the fabric into long strips, which he would use to bandage the wound. Jiri writhed about, whimpering.

"Finally, I can see something."

Otto eyed the wound closely.

"It didn't puncture your liver, luckily . . . nor your kidney. It isn't anything serious."

Jiri's eyes were wide with disbelief.

"You're just trying to console me. Oh, I know I'm dying. Friends, don't leave me here alone," he said in a theatrical tone.

"Stop that! You're not going to die. Not today, anyway. It's a surface wound; it sliced through your skin and a bit of muscle. It's going to hurt but it isn't going to kill you."

Jiri began to sob once again; whether it was out of relief or pain, they could not tell. He broke into a slurred incomprehensible litany that could have very well been either a theatrical number or a Yiddish prayer.

Moshe surveyed the room bleakly. Only he, Otto, Berkovitz, Myriam, and Jacek remained. Jiri was now wounded. Elias was dying.

"I'm tired," he said as he slid down to the floor. "Damn tired."

The adrenaline that had fueled them moments before had drained away. Moshe struggled to recall how it had all begun, and if they had actually dreamed of their own rebellion. The idea of escaping now seemed nothing more than a pathetic illusion. The only thing he knew to be true was that they would never leave there alive.

"In a short while, it will be daybreak," he announced wearily. "At this rate, maybe they won't need to shoot any of us."

0400 Hours

Oberscharführer Johann Schmidt, still in full uniform, was stretched out across the camp bed inside his small office that contained a chair, a telephone that sat atop a desk, and a small metal filing cabinet. He heaved a sigh. He wasn't permitted to undress. The *Sturmbannführer*'s orders had been very clear: he was not to be relieved of his post until the prisoners from Block 11 had announced a verdict. Alone, in the half-light, Schmidt grunted in discontent. He had grown up in the country; he was accustomed to waking up early in order to milk the cows and tend to the fields. He enjoyed the simple things. The Reichsführer had ordered that the Jews be exterminated. He obeyed those orders. It was a job just like any other. There were, of course, moments in which the job proved to be quite taxing; opening the doors to the showers, for instance, was a revolting sight. Before death consumed them, amid the screams and the pounding of their fists against the walls and the door for often ten minutes at a time, they vomited, defecated, and tried to scale the other prisoners in order to reach the residual oxygen that remained high above them. On one occasion, the Oberscharführer remembered having seen a corpse who had lodged two of his fingers inside the eye socket of another dead man. The sight of it had caused him to be sick. But the *Reichsführer* justified it as painful but necessary, and there was nothing else that could be done.

But he never could quite understand the commander's tortuous tactics. Those ten prisoners were going to be executed from the start, regardless of any concessions made. And even though the commander made every effort to thwart attempted escapes by way of drastic penalties, the camp was much too large to remain under the control of a few hundred SS. And so Breitner invented his vicious little games . . . at times, even on the ramp. He had seen the commander, welcoming the Jews with a smile as they climbed down from the trains and often apologizing to them for any discourtesy his officers might have shown. Afterward, never breaking from his same cordial manner, he would direct them toward the crematorium. And throughout his entire reception, he would give subtle close inspection to each of their faces, as if searching for something. On occasion, he would separate a little boy or girl from his or her parents, giving the pretext of a vaccination or perhaps to invite them to join the *Kinderheim.* He himself would usher the child away without protest from the mother or father; for they were certain that such a refined and educated officer would take great care in returning their child to them as quickly as possible. Instead, the children disappeared. Who knew where they ended up. Schmidt didn't want to know.

"It's all the commander's fault," he muttered to himself. His fault that, at this hour of the night, he was still confined to his post. He and the Jews were to blame.

Beneath his cot, he kept a bottle of liquor. He picked it up and held it a few inches from his face so he could read the label once more. Cognac. Unadulterated French cognac. He would never know how in the hell that rogue Moshe managed to get hold of a bottle of French cognac at camp. Kanada housed every imaginable treasure. Once there, the difficulty lay only in retrieving it. The damned spies in the SS security posts would have launched an inquiry even over a bottle of booze. As if work wasn't arduous enough—alcohol was indeed a necessary means of easing the drudgery.

Schmidt held firmly to the bottle, and with a turn of his hand, the cork popped, producing a sudden and inviting sound. In the small adjacent room, the others were fast asleep, a sleep induced mostly by a drunken stupor. No one would bother him.

The Oberscharführer lifted his head and took a long swig from the bottle. The heat of the cognac spread merrily from his throat to the rest of his body. Immediately, Schmidt felt better. It was just what he needed. Perhaps he would be forced to wait on the Jews for another hour or so, and without the booze, he wouldn't have managed it. The soldiers had what seemed an un-limited supply of schnapps at their disposal, but French cognac was something altogether different.

The warrant officer downed two or three more generous swigs. He was beginning to feel a lot better. The harsh realities of the camp dissolved from his thoughts, though his calm state was quickly ruptured by a sobering thought: he was not alone. The commander could call on him at any moment with one of his many odd requests.

He had endured enough for one day, Schmidt decided. With obvious effort, he stood up from the cot and leaned over to the telephone. He took a sheet of a paper from his desk and tore off a small scrap. With deft skill, he slid the paper through a slight aperture in the back of the black Bakelite apparatus. It was an old trick he had learned from his predecessor. The paper would muffle the blow of the anvil, allowing the telephone to emit only a muted vibration.

Schmidt returned to his cot, contented. He felt he ought to

close his eyes, if only for a moment. He needed the rest. The
night had been long and it wasn't over yet. He regretted having
beaten the rabbi, but there was nothing he could do. It was regulation.

The warrant officer took another gulp. He then corked the
bottle and placed it, out of view, under his bed. Still wearing his
boots, he stretched out on top of the bed and closed his eyes,
groggy from the alcohol.

Just ten minutes, he promised himself as he drifted off to
sleep, just ten minutes. . . .

With weary steps, Myriam crossed the barrack once more, past
the clothesline and into the darkness. Elias still lay unconscious.
She placed his hand in her own and gently caressed it. Jacek stood
aloof, near the window. Jiri was laid out across a mound of blankets. The bleeding had stopped. His brow was drenched in sweat,
presumably the result of a fever, yet his gaze was alert.

"Where did we leave off?" Berkovitz asked, as he kneaded the
area of his lower abdomen where he had been hit by Paul's boot.
One of his lenses had been cracked in the fight.

Moshe pointed to Otto. "He needed to escape, that's what I
recall at any rate."

"At this point, it's too late for me. I won't manage to infiltrate
within this morning's *Arbeitskommandos* unit. My comrades will
have fled without me. And even if we were to call the Oberscharführer, who would we name?"

Each of the prisoners looked toward the other.

"Perhaps there's another way out," Moshe spoke, exhausted.
"It's been on my mind for some time."

"What are you talking about?"

"We set the barrack on fire. We take the blankets and uniforms and make a heap, in the middle of the room so that the flame stays undetected for as long as possible. At this hour, there are very few guards on duty. The *Wäscherei* will be charred before they can manage to intervene. There'll be no shortage of confusion, and in the midst of it all, you can slip out the back."

Otto looked at his comrades with a crestfallen air.

"I can't let you do that. Even if I managed, what would happen to all of you? You'd end up in the bunker, dying of starvation."

"You don't need to worry. We'll tell them that the whole affair was your doing. That you threatened us with a knife. Besides, in the last few months, the jackboots haven't had the same vengeful approach they once did when it came to escapes. Two years back, they executed ten prisoners, but after the last incident, there wasn't a single death. The front line is closing in, and Breitner knows it."

"Moshe is right," Berkovitz said. "The commander knows his limitations."

"Don't entertain yourself with stories," Otto said with a sneer. "You know just what Breitner will do to us. And I'm not—"

"Listen to me!" Moshe snapped. "I'd rather go out this way. No matter what we do, there's no hope for us. And this way, Breitner can't force us into giving him a name. Elias was right—refusing to choose will be our victory."

"I'm with you," Jiri uttered with a sigh, unable to muster another word.

"Don't count me in," Jacek voiced from the far side of the room. "I'm not getting involved."

Otto, Moshe, and Berkovitz all turned. They saw that, in the midst of their distraction, Jacek had managed to grab hold of the knife.

"Now, that's rubbish," Moshe said, pointing in the direction of where Paul's body now lay on the floor. "You already *are* involved. You simply stood by when Otto . . . *stopped* Paul."

"If I manage to block your escape, then I won't be the one they're after. I'm calling the guards."

"No, you won't," Moshe said flatly.

"And who's going to stop me? There's only a few of you left. And I've got the knife."

"You won't go through with it. You're not that much of a fool. But what's more, I'd say that even you, Jacek, have a little heart. Tell the truth, wouldn't you like to pull one over on the jackboots? Wouldn't it make you laugh? It'd be like getting away with a hand goal. What do you say?"

"It'd be something," Jacek answered. "But I can't. I told you about my brother, I need to make it out of here alive for him."

"Even if that meant letting the rest of us die?"

Jacek gave no answer.

In the midst of the silence that had followed them, a faint voice could be heard. It was that of Jiri. His voice gained strength, though he stopped to catch his breath; he spoke without pretense, in his natural timbre, both deep and low.

"Your brother is gone, Jacek."

The *Blockältester* spun around with a look filled with both fury and suspicion.

"What did you say?"

"Your brother is gone, Jacek. I'm sorry." Mustering the strength to speak had all but exhausted him.

The barrack leader kneeled down beside him, gripping the knife so that the blade hung ominously over Jiri.

"What did you just say? You don't know anything."

"I know something that you don't. I'm sorry. I didn't want to have to tell you like this, but—"

Jacek stared, incredulous and frightened.

"I told you that, on occasion, I'd meet Wehrmacht, SS officers, and men from the RSHA." He paused to catch his breath. "At the bar where I worked there were always quite a few of them . . . they drank more than they should have done, and then they let themselves go. In bed, they talked and talked . . . they wanted to let off some steam, I suppose. And I'd listen. They became so unguarded. And for a moment, they forgot about their uniform and their Hitler."

"I don't care about any of this. They're just lies anyway."

"Listen to me, Jacek. Shortly before I was arrested, I found myself in the company of an Obersturmführer; blond, pale, very handsome." Jiri was covered in sweat. He pressed his hand into to his side in order to alleviate the pain. "He had come from a military raid. He recounted the whole affair to me. How they took the prisoners, where they sent them, what they— And even still, idiot that I was, I was assured I was safe there with him . . . he was tormented, you could see it. He hated himself for what he had done, but he knew he had no choice but to follow orders. And therein lies the trouble with Germans: they never disobey orders."

"Keep talking, fag. Let's see how many stories you can invent."

"The blond officer told me that, that evening, they had raided the house of a famous football player who had been arrested for his involvement in the black market—"

Jacek lunged toward Jiri, and with the palm of his hand smacked him across the face.

"Shut up, piece of shit Jew!"

With the back of his hand, Jiri wiped off the blood that now trickled down his chin.

"If you want, I'll stop. But I think you'd rather hear it. The blond told me that they had been in the footballer's apartment. One of the neighbors had called the police on account of what they believed was suspicious activity. When they entered; they found a boy there, confined to a wheelchair. He was missing both an arm and a leg . . ."

Jacek turned pale.

"Hidden inside the armoire was a Polish member of the AK. When he attempted to flee out the window, the officers didn't think twice but to shoot. Both at him and at the boy in the wheelchair. As he told the story, I could tell it made him want to cry. To kill a boy in cold blood, one confined to a wheelchair, without an arm or a leg, could not have been easy. The lieutenant said that the boy looked him in the eye even at the very end. He said that the boy was unafraid; knowing that bothered him most of all. He had no means of defending himself, and yet he was not afraid—"

"Shut up, you piece of shit Jew."

Jacek raised the knife, leaving it suspended above Jiri. For an instant, Moshe was convinced that the Pink Triangle would soon be the fourth victim that night. But Jacek's momentum slowed into an awkward swing. He let the knife fall to the floor and began to cry.

"If Breitner could see us now, he might not be so sure of himself," noted Moshe.

Jacek got up from the floor. With the sleeve of his jacket, he wiped his cheeks. He then retreated to the corner where he crouched upon the floor, and propping his head on his knees, he slowly and rhythmically rocked back and forth.

"Come on," Moshe urged the others, "I believe it's time for us to begin our bonfire."

Otto turned to Myriam. "Well, what do you say?"

Myriam crossed to Otto and flung her arms around him. "I hope you make it, Otto."

"I hope you all do too."

"All right then, is everyone ready?" asked Moshe.

"We'll need to move quickly. Pile up the sheets."

They gathered the blankets into a mound in the middle of the room.

"Just a second," Moshe said. "Add these."

He pulled the SS uniforms from the clothesline and threw them on the heap.

"They'll finally be put to good use," he said.

"Get ready, Otto. The moment the flames reach the walls, you'll have to move quickly if you're going to make it out of here. And remember, when the war is over, do what is honorable so that Germany will one day be a better place. Good luck."

The Red had been moving toward the door. But with those last words, he stopped and slowly turned to Moshe. He gestured as if to say something, but couldn't find the words to speak. With a puzzled look, he made his way toward the exit.

Using the same lighter he had used to sterilize the knife, Moshe sparked the lighter and moved the flame toward the heap. Just as he readied the flame, he heard Otto's voice.

"Moshe, wait."

The commander couldn't sit still. He paced back and forth in the half-light of the study. His eyes were transfixed upon the chessboard. A delirium had taken hold of him, as if the outcome of his the game was of great import.

The game had reached a most remarkable, unanticipated turning point. The black pawns were but a few moves away from infiltrating a small breach caused by the enemy's deployment tactics. They no longer moved as if they were a disjointed force, but rather like a skilled platoon of army reserves. It had been necessary to sacrifice the pawn and the rook, and yet, at the very end, they had still managed to attain the impossible. Breitner grabbed hold of a piece in preparation for the final move. A black pawn had infiltrated the board's opposing side and had transformed into a most fearsome and powerful queen.

Breitner fell into the armchair with a heavy sigh and leaned back. He was, at once, both bewildered and frightened. So it was possible for a worthless pawn, despite hundreds of obstacles, to prevail against a far more formidable enemy. Moreover, that it managed by itself and without help, at least for a moment, to turn the tide of the battle. The unyielding organization and the relationship of the forces within the camp mattered not. Nor did the superiority of their race, with all of its power and glory. Even within the boundless reaches of their supremacy, there was always the possibility that a single individual could change the course of history.

Breitner looked out over the KZ, which was still shrouded by the silence of the night. Could it be that, there within those walls, under his watchful eye, there in his own camp, one of his own pawns would transform into a queen?

He had received word from Berlin that very morning, alerting him that, in a few short weeks, hundreds of thousands of prisoners would arrive from Hungary. And just as all the others had, they too would disembark from the trains utterly unaware of what awaited them. Breitner felt overwhelmed by the task that awaited him. *Arbeitsvernichtung* . . . hundreds of thousands of people to annihilate by way of labor and incineration. He felt as if his task far exceeded not only that of the military, but all of the Reich. One of them—perhaps the strongest, most able-bodied of prisoners— would manage to survive, and that was all they needed to perpetuate their race.

In that moment, he knew with irrefutable certainty that defeat was inevitable. The Third Reich's dream would never be fulfilled. *Großdeutschland,* which was to stretch from the Ural Mountains as far as the Atlantic, would forever remain a dream. They had fought, exhausting themselves of all their strength and resources, until the very end, but their fate was inescapable. Breitner didn't imagine it, he didn't foresee the end, but he knew it was near. Perhaps someone in Berlin was already aware. Or perhaps, hidden in their bunkers, that reality eluded them, and victory still seemed within their reach. Goebbels fumed with rage on the front page of the newspaper, prophesying the onset of an imminent reversal of the front lines. Did he even believe it,

Breitner asked himself, or was he, too, aware that it was all nothing more than propaganda?

Even with the V-2s that battered London and the heavy water
trials now under way in Peenemünde, to any soldier it was evident that the war had been lost.

The telephone rang. The commander glanced instinctively at
the clock. It was nearly five. It had to be something of great importance. He eyed the phone as if willing it to stop ringing. But
the sound did not cease.

"Hello?" he demanded. His tone changed abruptly, and almost imperceptibly, his back straightened at attention.

"What? Yes, I understand. But. . . ."

A long silence followed.

"*Jawohl!* Understood. I will carry out the orders immediately.
Heil Hitler!"

He hung up the phone. For a moment he stood, staring into the
distance. When he had gathered his thoughts, he picked up the
receiver once more and dialed the number of the guards' station.
At least a minute passed as he waited impatiently for a response,
but his call went unanswered.

"Schmidt!" he shouted in aggravation, as he slammed the receiver down. "Where the hell are you?"

"Did you forget your bags?" Moshe asked.

Otto shifted away from the door and moved toward the others once again.

"Put the lighter away, for a moment at least."

Moshe reluctantly obliged.

"Listen, Moshe. I've thought this over." He stared at him fixedly. "You're the one who must escape."

"Me? It's your name on the ticket, not mine. You're the one who's supposed to change the fate of the world."

"And I believed that, too, at least until a moment ago. But what you said made me think."

"What did I say? Good luck?"

"You said, 'When the war is over, do what is honorable so that Germany will one day be a better place.' And you were right. My comrades and I aim to liberate the party, and in turn, perhaps we'll be able to organize an internal resistance in Germany to combat the Reich. And when the war is over at last, we will fight to ensure that such horrors never happen again."

"And as stratagems go, does that not suffice?"

"It's worthy of our efforts, there is no doubt . . . but it is a goal that speaks of the future. It will be thanks to us and many others that Germany will one day be a better place, and yet, all of you will not be alive to witness it. I represent that future, but it is the present that needs us in this moment."

Moshe looked over at his remaining comrades.

"We're a battered lot."

Otto's eyes brimmed with emotion.

"But you're here! You're alive! And in Hungary, there are hundreds of thousands of Jews, who, in a not too distant future, will end up here only to be executed. We must stop them; they must be warned! The Americans must attack the crematoriums. It must be done without delay. Don't you see? You cannot discard the present for the future. It would be an injustice."

"But you could be the one—"

"And how exactly? Should I saunter over to the Americans and explain the current situation? I'm a Communist; they'll detect it right away. They won't listen to me. I am not the right person. That person is you."

"You're mistaken. You're the hero here."

"Listen to me, Moshe. Within these walls, I've learned one thing: when the odds are against you saving everyone, you must first save those who will assuredly save others. And in here, you're our only hope. We all know that soon the jackboots will be infiltrating Hungary. How many of you are there? A million? A million and a half? Nazis are an efficient breed. At this point, they're sending ten thousand a day through the crematorium. We have no time to lose."

"And so you thought of me."

"You'll be the one to escape. My comrades will come to your aid. When they find you hidden away in the ditch, they'll know that I sent you. No one else knows of it."

"All right. But come with me then."

"I can't. In the ditch there is only space for three; in truth, not even: you'll be forced to lay flat, each on top of the other. There is no space for movement. It will be far from comfortable; confined for days in that space, you'll end up pissing yourself."

"I can't say I imagined a five-star resort."

"My comrades are Polish; once you make it out, they'll see to it that you survive. Relay to them all that has happened and inform them that you have been given a new mission. You are safe in their hands, of this I can assure you. Tell them the word, *Dombrowski*; they will understand."

"Dombrowski . . . in which barrack was he?"

Otto smiled. "He was a general in the Paris Commune. We chose his name as a code word. My Polish comrades will pass you off as Belarusian or something of the sort. All that matters is that no one suspects you of being a Jew; here in Poland it's far too dangerous. The AK will help you reach Slovenia, and from there, you can make your way into Hungary. It's there that you'll fight for your cause."

"But I don't know if—"

"You *must*. The fate of the Hungarian people depends upon you. They would never believe in me. But in you, a Jew from Warsaw, they would, undoubtedly. Your voice will be heard. Go to your communities and your rabbis and tell them all that is about to befall them. They will help you prevent further horrors. And in America, too, there are a great many of you. But it is you who must go."

"You've won me over," Moshe said ironically. "As soon as the magic carpet arrives, I'll be on my way."

"But you must at least try! Moshe, stop playing the part of the disillusioned cynic for once. You're the one who must escape tonight."

Moshe scanned the room, surveying who remained of his

imprisoned companions: Otto, a German; Jacek, a Polish criminal; Jiri, a homosexual who compromised himself by conceding
to the whims of the SS officers; Berkovitz, a double-crossing financier; and Myriam, a woman.

"Yours is the only card that can trump all the others," Otto
asserted.

Moshe heaved a sigh. He felt so very tired. . . .

"I'm not strong like you, Otto."

"You are much stronger. Because now you have a cause."

Without permitting him a moment to protest, the Red ush-
ered him in the direction of the door.

"Give me the lighter."

After a moment's hesitation, Moshe handed it to him.

"Wait."

They all turned to Jacek. The former footballer was seated on
the floor, staring steadfastly at the others. His face bore a feverish
expression.

"I can help," he said.

"There's no need, Jacek. Just don't get in our way."

"But I want to help you. I'll do everything in my power to
ensure that Moshe escapes alive." The barrack leader's eyes glim-
mered wildly. His cheekbones were swollen from the earlier
fight, but his face radiated with an energy that could only denote
a return of enthusiasm. "Swear to me that you will never get
caught. That you will persist despite the dangers, for us and for
my brother."

Moshe gave a solemn nod.

"A fire is smart," Jacek began, "but it won't suffice. You'll still
have to find a way past the electric fences. So, while the fire oc-
cupies the guards, I'll sneak into the depot; I know a way in. If
I'm spotted by any of the SS, I'll say that there's an *Arbeitskommando* scheduled to begin shortly. Regardless, we haven't much

time before the reveille. As for the wall, having worked with the
electricians at camp more than a time or two, I know the layout
perfectly. Moreover, I know how to trigger a short circuit. We'll
need clippers and rubber gloves. There is an isolated dark spot.
We can cut the barbed wire and you can escape to the hideout."

"You don't have to do that—"

"I *want* to," he quickly countered. "After the wires have been
severed, I'll find a way to distract the guards stationed nearby.
Moshe, your cigarettes might do the trick."

Moshe promptly pulled out the pack that had been hidden in
the folds of his jacket and handed them to Jacek.

"It will be dangerous."

Jacek gave only a shrug. "You have to remember, I'm a defender. My job is to block any adversary while the forwards try
to score a goal."

"Get ready," Otto said, turning to Moshe.

"As soon as the flames hit the ceiling, jump out of the rear
window. Jacek will leave with you. He'll help you scale the wall.
Make your way toward Mexico; there you'll find the mound."
He grabbed a pencil and mapped out the plan on one of the scraps
of paper.

"You'll find it here," he said, drawing an X. "You can't miss
it. Is it clear?"

Moshe gave a nod. Otto smiled and then chewed the paper,
destroying the map.

"In a few short hours, my comrades will join you."

Moshe nodded. The world seemed to be spinning around
him; his brain felt as if it had stopped working.

Otto crouched near the base of the heaped linens. At that very
moment, a chill coursed through the air.

"Daybreak," Moshe whispered under his breath. The others,
consumed by the same thought, turned toward the window.

With that, Otto eyed him with a smile.

"We have to hurry."

"Just a second," answered Moshe. He crossed to Myriam and pulled her into his arms. She stood, passively wrapped in his embrace.

"Don't give up," he whispered. "You mustn't give up no matter what lies ahead. For Ida. Remember that she may still be out there."

He then turned toward the others.

"I suppose you needn't wait up for me. I might be a bit late."

Otto moved the lighter to the base of the mound of linens and lit the flame.

0500 Hours

"*Jawohl*, Herr Kommandant!" a drowsy voice finally greeted him from the other end of the telephone line.

"Herr Oberscharführer!" Breitner barked. "Where have you been? I've been looking for you for more than half an hour! I demand an explanation."

"I had gone—" The warrant officer searched in vain for words in his bleary state. "I had gone to inspect the situation at the washhouse. All is in order, Herr Sturmbannführer!"

"I expect you to draw up a full report first thing tomorrow morning," ordered Breitner. The warrant officer's sleepy voice had not gone unnoticed.

"Have you orders for me, Herr Sturmbannführer?"

"Send them to the wall, Herr Oberscharführer. Take them to the wall and have them executed. Every one of them. Immediately."

"But, Commander, you had said—"

Breitner didn't let him finish.

"The previous orders have been revoked. I am now arranging for the prisoners to be shot. All of them, have I made myself clear?

Los! I want to hear shots fired within ten minutes. Afterward, take them to the crematorium, immediately."

He hung up the phone.

He knew what he had to do. During that final hour in which he waited for Schmidt to answer the telephone, he had planned his every move.

He exited the office and made his way toward the bedroom. Frieda was sleeping. On her face was a serene expression. Next to her lay Felix; he was dressed in a pair of pajamas that he had now outgrown. As usual, the little boy, having noted his father's absence, had crept into his parents' bed and fallen fast asleep.

For a moment, Breitner stood, lost in thought. They were so lovely. Lovely and innocent. If there was still a way that he could spare them the horrors, he would need to move quickly.

Breitner knelt down next to his wife and softly whispered: "Frieda, Frieda, wake up."

She opened her eyes. When she focused upon him, she broke into a smile. She was not afraid, even despite seeing that her husband had woken her at dawn, for she had long learned to trust in him.

"Karl, what is it?" she whispered so as not to wake the child.

"Quickly, you must get up."

For the first time, a shadow of worry passed over his wife's face.

"Did something happen?" she asked as she sat up, revealing her pristine nightgown and placing her bare feet upon the floor.

"Berlin telephoned." He hesitated to carry on. He hadn't the courage to continue.

"And?" Frieda stared unwaveringly, her eyes filled with dread. Every trace of sleep had evaporated from her face. Breitner cast his eyes away from her.

"They are transferring me." He faltered. "I have to leave for the Russian front. It's effective immediately. Within two or three days, a new commander will arrive to take my place."

"But they can't! You have always—"

"The orders arrived from the Reichsführer himself. I cannot contest them."

"But you have worked so hard. Here at camp you've—"

"There's nothing to be done, don't you see, Frieda? Now, we must think only of ourselves, and more important, of Felix."

The commander's wife turned instinctively toward her son, whose slumber carried on uninterrupted.

"Nothing is going to happen to you, I can promise you that, but you will have to leave right away."

"I'll stay with you. How will you manage?"

"No, I'm telling you that you cannot stay. There's nothing to discuss. I'll call for the car and will wake the driver. You could leave this very morning. Can you manage it?"

Frieda looked about the room in confusion. In that moment, she had lost all sense of security.

"But what about us . . . how will we manage without you? I—"

"Listen to me, Frieda." Breitner took a seat next to her on the bed. He took her hand. The mattress' movement caused Felix to stir. With a slight sigh, he turned to face the other side. With a hushed but resolute tone, the commander spoke.

"I will telephone one of the bigwigs in Berlin. I'll have some false documents prepared so that you can safely enter Switzerland. When you arrive in Zurich, there is an account under my name; there is plenty of money for you there."

His words seemed to comfort Frieda.

"But where do I go? And how will I get it?"

"I'll explain everything. But listen to me, it's important. We must do this for Felix, understood? There is no future for him in Germany."

Before Frieda could speak, he placed his finger upon her lips.

"The Americans and Russians will raze everything to the ground. Do you remember what happened after Versailles? They will have control of everything once again. It is for this reason that you must take him away from here. Take him far away from these horrors. So that he might have a chance."

The thought was devastating to Frieda. Her world was crumbling before her.

"But where will we go? And how will we manage?"

"Go to South America. As soon as you can; take refuge there. I have friends who will help you. I'll send you a list of names to contact in Argentina; they have already been alerted."

"And what about you?"

"I will join you as soon as I can."

Frieda's lower jaw quivered; she couldn't hold back her tears.

"Karl . . . oh, Karl . . ." She fell into his arms, holding him tightly.

"I know it hurts. But Felix deserves this. He isn't to blame for all of this; poor Felix is innocent. And so he should remain. Tell him nothing. He must never know anything about all of this."

"But then how can I . . . how will I explain all of this?"

"Invent something, tell him whatever you like. But do not speak of me, or you, or of the camp. The less he knows the better off he will be. He's safer this way; you understand that, don't you? He will have only his future ahead of him, and no past to hinder him."

They remained in each other's embrace for a long while, each in an effort to comfort the other. A sudden flash of light caught their attention in the half-light of the room. The commander rushed to the window, flinging open the curtains.

The washhouse was engulfed in flames.

"Hello, *libling,* darling, come in. I've nearly finished. What did the rabbi say?"

He scanned the room. His wife was dusting a picture frame, one that held an old and somewhat grainy black-and-white photograph of a pale little girl with long blond braids.

"He sends his regards," he answered as he took off his coat. "And he says that one should focus not on the past but the future . . . the future, you see? For us, the future might only mean next week."

He put on his glasses and sat down at the little table in the den where an enormous half-completed puzzle lay. Hundreds of pieces were scattered around it, heaped into small piles according to color. The old man took one at random, surveyed the puzzle at length, and then attempted to fit the piece into a few different positions. Having no luck, he huffed with aggravation and tossed the piece to the side. He then cast his gaze across the room to his wife.

"How can I not think about the past? More than fifty years have passed, and not a day goes by that I don't think about it. According to him, I should just forget having escaped from camp. It

was all for nothing . . . not even a single Jew in all of Hungary
was saved, and all because . . . all because . . ."

"Calm down. Don't think about that."

"All that I did, the documents that I brought, the registries,
the testimonies . . . and none of did any good! It was all for nothing. The rabbis and the community leaders spent weeks sending
my reports out to one another. They even mailed one to the Pope!
The absurdity of it all! I can only imagine what they thought he
would do."

"You needn't slight the—"

"At any rate, the jackboots had already invaded and begun
their cleansing tactics. Those that could bought their own salva-
tion in Switzerland. Ugh, how despicable it all was! And even we
were—"

"Please don't start this, *libling*, I beg you—"

"But we too are to blame, we *survived*, and I'll never forgive
myself for it."

He fell silent, tormented by his thoughts. The woman offered
a gentle caress, for it was, in truth, the only way to calm him.

"It's almost time for lunch."

He heaved a sigh. His eyes returned to the colossal puzzle
before him.

"Perhaps I should have bought the child's version, you know,
the ones with the twenty-five gargantuan pieces. As it is, I can't see
anything anyway. Do you think they make puzzles in Braille?"

She laughed softly as she made her way back to the kitchen.

The man, whose glasses had slid past the bridge to the tip of
his nose, took to studying the pieces once again. His strategy involved taking a piece, examining it with the intensity and precision a stonecutter might employ before attempting to wedge the
piece into a series of a niches; if that approach failed, he would

simply set the it aside. In a few short minutes, he had managed to position five pieces.

The doorbell rang.

"Who could that be?" he asked, though he made no sign of leaving his chair.

"I don't know," she answered in a voice that carried a faint hint of disquietude. "We weren't expecting anyone today."

"We're *never* expecting anyone."

"I'll go and see."

"Be careful. There have been some shady figures in this area for some time now."

"What would burglars come looking for here?"

"I don't mean burglars; I'm talking about politicians: the elections are not far off. I've heard they're making their rounds going to each and every door. Just be careful."

She turned away from her husband as her face broke into a smile.

"If they ask for your vote," he carried on from his seat in the den, "tell them that we would gladly give our support but our grandchildren simply won't allow it."

"I'll have a look before I unhook the chain, don't worry."

The woman slid the chain within its clasp and opened the door. A man in his sixties was at the door; he was tall and robust, with piercingly blue eyes that emitted a penetrating stare and blond hair that had receded ever so slightly. He wore a lightweight blue suit.

The woman stared, surprised by the sight.

"Can I help you?"

Her question caused the stranger to react oddly. His face became flushed; the large, looming figure suddenly appeared awkward, even timid.

"I . . . forgive me . . ." The words eluded him. His voice carried a barely discernible accent, from South America perhaps.

The woman looked on curiously. She was sure that he had the wrong address.

"Can I come in?"

She hesitated a moment.

"Forgive me, I'm not sure that we've ever met before. Who are you looking for?"

"I was hoping to find—" he gathered the strength to speak "—Moshe Sirovich and his wife, Myriam. Do I have the right address?"

The old woman was bewildered.

"Yes. But . . ."

She stared, perplexed.

"Can I come in?" the man asked again. "It's rather important."

"*Libling*, what is it? Who's at the door?" Moshe called from his seat in the den.

She turned toward her husband.

"A man . . . he wants to speak to us . . ."

"Well then, as long as he's not a tax collector, let him in."

Myriam unclasped the chain and swung open the door.

"Please, come in."

The blond man stood awkwardly, his hands fidgeted nervously.

"Come into the den. Here, this is my husband."

Moshe turned toward their guest.

"Forgive me if I don't get up, but at my age, I've got to conserve energy."

The man stood motionless, still obviously ill at ease.

"What are you waiting for, a formal invitation? Sit. We don't have much to offer, just some tea if you'd like."

The man politely declined. He took a seat in a worn, cracked leather armchair situated just across from Moshe. With a nod from her husband, Myriam, too, took a seat. Her apprehension was evident.

"Good," the old man said, "Whoever you are, we're pleased to have you; if anything, you'll be a nice distraction. Now, why is it that you've come?"

The blond man looked imploringly to Moshe; he was so overcome that he couldn't speak.

"You needn't worry," said Moshe. "We'll start with something simple, like your name, perhaps."

The colossal man seemed paralyzed with fright; he made a great effort to speak.

"My name is Breitner. Felix Breitner."

Moshe's complacent expression became, at once, shrouded in uncertainty. His smile vanished from his face.

"We don't know any Breitner."

"My father was Karl Breitner."

Moshe's turned ashen; Myriam held her breath with fright.

"Breitner? You're *that* Breitner?"

At that, Moshe's body shook with rage. He heaved himself from his chair and stood, looming over the man, who suddenly seemed quite small. The muscles in his neck and jaw were pulled taut.

"Leave!" he ordered. "Leave this house immediately."

The gargantuan man trembled; he opened his mouth in attempts to give some sort of explanation, but when only silence accompanied him, he gave up. He gathered his nerves and stood from his chair. In the frigid silence that hung about the room, he turned and headed toward the door. Myriam found the strength to escort their guest to the door. Moshe remained behind, immobile.

Felix Breitner opened the door himself. He walked through the doorway, and stopping midway, he turned toward Myriam. With a quick gesture, he pulled an envelope from his jacket and handed it to Myriam.

"I only wanted to give you this."

Myriam took the envelope though she did not open it. She could not bring herself to look at the man in her doorway.

"Leave." Her voice was strained. "Leave now."

She closed the door, collapsing against it with labored breathing. Tears ran down her cheeks. After a moment, she locked every latch and bolt, and then, with the back of her hand, she dried her eyes.

Returning to the den, she found Moshe, still in the very same position; he looked as if some divine force had turned him into a pillar of salt. She wrapped her arms around him, instantly breaking the spell. Though she had revived him, Moshe spoke not a word.

It was only when his gaze fell upon her hands that he finally spoke.

"What's that?" he asked, pointing to the bag that Myriam now held in her right hand. She had nearly forgotten about it.

"He gave it to me."

Moshe took hold of the envelope; he turned it around in his hands, but had not the resolve to open it. He feared its contents, for no matter its size, the envelope was big enough to hold the past.

After a moment, he decided to look. He slid one finger inside and eyed the contents.

A photograph.

He pulled the image from the envelope so that only a sliver was visible. Myriam watched, her eyes urging him to continue.

Moshe gripped the corner, and with his thumb and index finger, he pulled out the photograph.

They gasped at the sight.

The photograph was of a grave. It was a black-and-white image, taken at close range.

The grave was unassuming, just a simple light gray headstone in what seemed to be, though it was barely visible, a churchyard cemetery. Behind it, a small gravel path led to a gate in the distance.

At the base of the grave sat a vase filled with a bouquet of flowers.

There was a photograph on the headstone.

Myriam clapped a hand over her mouth to stifle her cries.

Moshe, too, his eyes wide, dropped open his jaw, though no sound came forth. A moment passed and he found the strength to speak.

"Ida . . ."

Myriam rushed to the window. She opened it and leaned out as far as she could.

The blond man was already crossing the street; he was nearly thirty yards away. He walked with the haste of a man escaping.

"Wait!" she cried out as loudly as she could. "Wait!"

A soft wind shook the branches of the birch trees. The valleys were dotted with daisies and poppies, the first flowers of the season. The sky was bright and clear, and the sun's rays warmed the air pleasantly. It was a splendid day in the eastern German countryside.

Just outside the entrance of a quaint cemetery, Myriam and Moshe lingered for a moment. They stared resolutely at the iron gate, though they had not yet resolved to go through it. They were both dressed in dark colors. Moshe's suit hung limply about him; the sleeves were too long; he had bought it many years ago for a friend's funeral. It had hung in the armoire for many years until now. On his head, he wore a *kippah*. Myriam's long-sleeved dress was decorated with lace trim that fell about her wrists, which gave her a youthful air. Next to them, at a distance of a few steps, stood Felix in his customary blue suit. He looked on shyly.

An empty street lined the entrance of the cemetery. In the parking lot, whose white stripes shone in the daylight, sat one small blue car. A few miles to the east, one could make out the humble silhouette of a little hillside village. Only a few hours earlier, they had met Felix Breitner again, after having seen him in New York. After more than fifty years, they had returned to Germany.

"So, this is it," Moshe said.

"It's all that I could do. I know that it isn't much, but—"

"No," Myriam interjected with a smile. "For us it means so very much. This is important to us. There is not a nicer gift that you could have given us."

Felix, not knowing quite what to do, stood wringing his hands.

"Eh, well, I . . ."

"What would your father say?" Moshe asked. "That is, if he were around today."

The tall blond man lowered his gaze.

"I don't know. I never really knew my father. I hadn't even a single memory of him until"—he put one hand in his pocket—"until these came."

Fishing through the pockets of his jacket, he pulled out the contents. They were chess pieces. Moshe and Myriam looked on, puzzled.

"Here. You see?"

Felix lifted the pawn. At the base of the piece, the name *Jan* had been written. He then turned over the knight. At that point, Moshe found himself reading his own name aloud. The queen's piece read *Myriam*.

"I don't understand . . ."

"All of the sudden, I began to remember everything about that night. My mother had never wanted to talk about it. She never told me why we had to flee Germany, nor did she ever explain what had happened to my father. Her stories were always vague regarding that night. But those chess pieces brought me back to that night, and now I remember it perfectly clearly."

Moshe and Myriam looked on in disbelief.

"That night, the night when you escaped from camp, my father and I were playing chess. I was eight years old then."

"The same age as Ida," Myriam spoke softly, overcome by the memory.

"Chess bored me a great deal back then, and so I asked my father if we could give the pieces names."

"Our names . . ."

"At the time, I had no idea. Not yet anyway. And then, the very next morning, my mother and I left. I had forgotten about that night until a year ago, when a box of my father's personal effects was sent to me. During the last few months of the war, he was shipped to the front lines and was later captured by the Russians. I still don't know how he spent his last days or how he died. His belongings were sequestered and shipped to a warehouse in East Germany. After the Wall fell, they began cataloging old relics which they then shipped back to their legitimate owners."

"Incredible."

"And so, I received the chess pieces. And suddenly, I remembered everything. I began to research the camp; at the Auschwitz State Museum I discovered that our last night there was the very

same night of the revolt of the prisoners from Block Eleven. The
prisoners had set fire to the washhouse. I began to think that
there must have been a connection between the revolt and the
escape, that of my own and my mother's, the following morning.
As luck would have it, at Auschwitz I found the registry with all
of the names of the prisoners from the bunker. And I discovered
that the names of the *Häftlinge* who rioted that night were the
same as those written on the bottom of the chess pieces. And so,
I began to search for anyone, anywhere in the world, who might
have survived Block Eleven. It was not easy to find you."

"Your father—" Moshe began, though before he could carry
on, his voice broke.

"I know," Felix said. "I know everything now. I know how
terrible he was. But . . ."

"I know; he will always be your father," offered Myriam reassuringly.

"Together with the chess pieces, there was also a file, wasn't
there?" Moshe asked. "The one that you showed to us in New
York?"

Felix nodded.

"My father would select children at the ramp that he believed
could pass for Aryan. All blond-haired and blue-eyed. He would
then entrust them to families whom he knew. It was an experiment in Aryanization. He was convinced that, if given the proper
environment, he could override Jewish heredity and replace it
with that of the German race. He was nothing but a madman, I
know."

"Yes, perhaps," said Myriam. "But in doing so, he saved Ida
from the crematorium."

"But unfortunately—"

"We knew that Ida was already quite ill. My only hope is that
those last few months were peaceful for her."

With Felix still standing before them, they looked on in silence. No longer knowing what to say, Felix cast his eyes to the ground. Then, all at once, his gaze shot upward toward Myriam.

"It was the only thing I could do to ask for your forgiveness."

In silence, Moshe and Myriam walked through the gate and entered the cemetery.

"I'll wait for you here."

Almost upon entering, they found the headstone with Ida's picture, the same photograph that they had seen in New York. The grave looked just like all the hundreds of others that surrounded it. A woman wearing a brown headscarf appeared at the entrance. For a moment, they watched her. She followed the little gravel path into the cemetery, and then turned left off the path into the rows of headstones. She stopped in front of one of the many graves and placed a small bundle of flowers into a tarnished brass vase. With her head bowed, she began to pray, her lips moving ever so slightly.

Moshe and Myriam turned to the headstone once again. It didn't matter that they found themselves in a Catholic cemetery. It mattered only that they had found Ida.

Etched into the marble was a name and date: IDA SCHNEIDER 1936–1946. Nothing else. The name was not the same. But as for the photograph, there could be no doubt. It was Ida.

Moshe pulled a small knife from his pocket, and with it, cut a small strip off his jacket and placed it on the headstone. Myriam did the same.

And for a while, they prayed together; in soft voices, they offered their prayers in Yiddish. And only when they began to feel the heat of the sun as it reached its midpoint in the sky did they ready themselves to leave.

Just as Moshe began to make his way toward the gate, he felt a hand brush against his back. He turned around.

Behind him, gathered silently in a semicircle, stood the others. The prisoners of Block 11.

There was Otto: in his striped uniform, with his strong and solid frame, his eyes burning with drive and vigor. There was Jiri, bearing his same ironic expression, his body folded into its habitual ambiguous pose. There was Berkovitz, serious, remorseful, his metal-rimmed glasses glimmering in the sunlight. There was Elias, with his hands together as if in prayer and his eyes fixed on them. There was Jan, old and in poor health just as he had been that night, but still with enough strength to stand. There was Jacek, too, tall and lanky with ashen skin. And even Alexey, his eyes still showed his eternal rage. And at the back, just to the right, stood Paul, in his leather jacket and boots, with a brazen look about him. There they were, all of them together. All of the prisoners from Block 11. They looked on in silence while the wind swept through the valley, ruffling their hair and rustling their clothes. And then it happened. One by one, a smile broke across each of their faces. Jiri was the first, flashing but a hint of irony in his eyes. And then Otto, his teeth still strong and white. Then came Jan, Jacek, Paul, and Elias, and at last even Berkovitz and Alexey, even they smiled, perhaps for the first time. Their smiles evoked the same gentle sweetness that one might feel upon finding a friend after many long years.

"What's the matter? Aren't you coming?" Myriam asked, already a few steps ahead. "Did you see something?"

Moshe turned to his wife, shaking his head.

"No. It was nothing. Just a memory."

Jiri survived. His Prominenten *friends saw to it that he recovered in the camp hospital. He remained at the* Revier *until Poland was liberated, thus escaping the "death march," in which the prisoners were transferred to other internment camps. On January 27 of the following year, he found himself in the company of a Russian platoon, who welcomed him as one of their own. A few months later, he settled in Moscow, where he found a little work at the Bolshoi. In 1951, he married an opera singer with an ambiguous past life who was with child. He was struck down and killed by a bus while crossing the street on the way to the hospital to see his newborn.*

    Otto was incarcerated in the Stehzelle *of one of the bunkers for eight days. Myriam, however, was kept there only three days before being transferred to work in one of the factories at Buna. Despite being subjected to numerous torturous bouts on the Boger swing, he never gave the names of his accomplices nor did he disclose the means by which they escaped. Nevertheless, the new commander did not feel it necessary to have him executed: the Russians were advancing and he thought it ill-advised to antagonize the Resistance. A month later, Otto found his own escape; he crept away from the* Arbeitskommando *in which he had been working. He joined the forces of the Polish Army and fought against the Nazis just outside of the camp, using expeditious guerrilla warfare tactics. After the war, he returned to Germany, where he became an influential member of the Communist Party. He was twice elected to Parliament, but his harsh stance on matters of the regime caused him to separate from the party. On March 22, 1975, he was kidnapped just outside his home by men dressed in civilian clothing, who were most likely members of the STASI. His body was never found.*

    Despite his involvement in the escape, Berkovitz managed to survive. After being incarcerated for three days at the bunker, the governor's office telephoned the commander, recommending that the financier's life be spared. His friendships with the affluent had finally paid off. Berkovitz was transferred to the camp's kitchen, by far the best Kommando *that one could hope for: in the warmth with a limitless food supply at his disposal. In January of 1945, during the evacuation of the KZ, he managed to flee into the surrounding countryside and with the help of a Polish family, he was able to hide out in their nearby farm. A few months later, with the aid of the*

Red Cross, he was reunited with his family, along with his gold, in Switzerland. From that point, using his finances along with the generous proceeds from other wealthy financiers, he began conducting investigations to uncover and capture Nazi criminals across the globe. According to a number of unpublished reports, he played a crucial role in the capture of Adolf Eichmann. He followed every hearing of the war criminal's court case until Eichmann was condemned to death. According to some, he even personally assisted in the hanging. Berkovitz passed away in his sleep in 1973; he was cared for and tended to by his wife until the very end.

Jacek escaped from the barrack together with Moshe. He succeeded in triggering a short circuit and was able to cut the wires along the wall. As Moshe fled into the surrounding fields, he was spotted by an SS officer who extracted his pistol and took aim. Jacek lunged at the officer and threw him to the ground. Another soldier arrived at the scene and struck Jacek with the blunt end of his rifle, fracturing his skull. By then, Moshe had disappeared into the pale light of dawn. Jacek died a few hours later. He never regained consciousness. His body was burned in the crematorium. That was his last, and perhaps, most victorious defensive play.

Acknowledgments

I would first like to thank Auschwitz survivor Nedo Fiano for having the patience to explain the real living and working conditions of the camp, and for having been kind enough to have read this novel. I must also thank Paola Caccianiga, whose continual, invaluable guidance aided in the creation of both the characters and the storyline. Thanks to Vicki, who offered unwavering support for what initially seemed an unlikely project. And thanks to Rossella, an uncompromising critic, for whose honesty I am most indebted.

Extensive research was carried out in the drafting of this novel, though it is possible—probable, in fact—that there are inaccuracies or errors within the text. In this regard, I hope that I have not offended the reader; in case I have, I offer my humblest apologies. In an effort to justify any discrepancy, I can say that I drew upon the theme of *Shoah* with a reverent respect for mankind's greatest tragedy in history.

Glossary

AK: Armia Krajowa, clandestine army of the Polish Resistance

Appellplatz: central square in the concentration camp where daily roll call took place

Arbeitskommando: group of prisoners selected to perform special labor tasks

Blockältester: prisoner appointed by SS officers to oversee a block

Buna: camp factory within Auschwitz used for synthetic rubber and fuel production

Boger: former SS officer; infamous for methods of torture devised while at camp

Generalgouvernement: name given to German-occupied parts of Poland not given to the Reich

Green Triangle: criminal prisoner

Häftlinge: prisoners

HKB: Häftlingskrankenbau; a hospital for inmates

Ka-Be (KB): Krankenbau; common hospital located at the Buna concentration camp

Kapo: prisoner in charge of a group of inmates; foreman

Kanada: area within Auschwitz-Birkenau where prisoners' belongings were temporarily stored before being handed over to the Reich

Kremchy: (Origin: Russian) crematorium

Lagerältester: prisoner appointed by the SS to oversee a whole camp

Lagerkapos: Kapo in charge of the whole camp

Oberscharführer: staff sergeant

Pink Triangle: homosexual prisoner

Pipel: young boy utilized or exploited by the Kapos

Prominenten: powerful prisoners who had advantages, such as food or clothes

Red Triangle: political prisoner

Reichsführer: general of German Army and chief of the SS

Revier: common hospital

RSHA: Reich security main office

Ruhr: river in western Germany; a tributary of the Rhine

Sturmbannführer: major

Wasserraum: washhouse

Wehrmacht: German armed forces in the Third Reich